Enter My Imagination

JOHN P ALBA

A Shield Blade Publishing Book

https://sbpub.great-site.net/

Copyright © 2025 by John P Alba

ISBN: 978-0-9906878-6-3

Cover Design by John P Alba
Substantive and Copy Editing by TL Jeffcoat

DEDICATION

To my family and friends for the encouragement to finally
put my imagination on paper.

CONTENTS

FORWARD

There are fewer things scarier than I, one of those things is my Imagination, and the other is the willingness with which I let "It" loose upon the world... In life, we must choose our own paths, and sometimes we learn that all the things we have chosen are not the best things for us, so if you decide to go any further, then you choose to at your own risk and assume all and any risks involved upon entering through my "Door". YOU HAVE BEEN WARNED!! About me: I consider myself a storyteller, rather than a writer or an author, because I prefer not to be limited by my thoughts. I was born about nine months after I was created; I lived during my lifetime and will die at the end. I have many memories of my life and the scars to prove it. Upon my death, I will have lived a very long time, but not long enough. I have been both blessed and cursed by life. Through my actions and my words, I will live longer than most. On a personal note, about the way I tell a story, it is difficult for me to understand how to write "correctly" like a "Professional Writer" because I do not see the "errors" I put down on paper like "normal people" do. How is it that I "write incorrectly" if my dreams, my thoughts, and my imagination are the ones telling me what to write? If I can understand what they are saying, then how is it incorrect? Here is another example of what I see wrong with writing: if the typical conversation between two people were typed up, it would be considered incorrect writing. So, who decides what is well written or not? According to Editors and other sources, you need a beginning, middle, and an ending! Then explain to me the Twilight Zone! So how does that work in the world of normal? In my "world," what you call "normal," I call "common," and I am not a "common" person in any form or fashion. My mind asks me this type of question at 11:30 pm at night, "You are given three wishes, but one is to undo whatever you wished for. Meaning that if a wish goes awry and you want to undo it, you have the one wish in reserve to undo it, but if you do invoke it, the first two will be undone no matter what. Then you will start where you began, with no wishes, but you will have some knowledge of what that is; that is up to the individual. My Imagination is CRAZY.

i

SNEAKY ANGELS

It has been a while since I last wrote in my journal. Life has been loud since I moved back to the city and returned to school. The job is constant clattering pans, barking orders, the hiss of hot grease in the kitchen, and I have been buried in it. I have not stopped fighting demons, but not the metaphorical things that therapists babble about. The ones that leave scars on your soul and whisper sweet promises of release through cracked mirrors. Demons that trickle out of hell through those same cracks.

I wanted some meaning in life, more than just surviving. I never regretted the path I chose, but I knew it would not be easy. When I had the chance to walk away, I did not take it. No reason presented itself until now.

This might be my last entry. I am starting a new path, and I am not sure where to begin. Maybe from the moment I knew I was looking for a way out...

The thought first came to me at nine in the morning, after the second bell rang. I sank into my seat and ignored the cold and cracked vinyl beneath me. The professor walked in, grinning as if he had just won the lottery. If his grin had been any wider, I would have made plans to slay the demon inside him later.

"A surprise happy test," he said, voice syrupy and yet condescending. "Let's see what your soft, spongy brains have absorbed."

The test dragged on for an hour, each tick of the clock a hammer to my temples. The rest of the day unraveled with dull lectures and fluorescent lights that buzzed in my skull.

By three, I stumbled into the afternoon daylight, blinking against the glare. My head throbbed. My stomach churned. I walked to a kitchen down the street from the community college building I was working in, each step dragging across the pavement. My life became routine and boring. Even the last demon I faced was nothing more than a slobbering, pathetic thing feeding off a regular guy suffering from depression. Where do you go after saving the world when everything now feels so trivial?

The pub was a furnace. Fryers hissed and spat. The air reeked of scorched oil and sweat. The evening was worse than the day in class. I dropped two baskets of bread, and a football team came in like a pack of wolves, ordering wings until everyone in the kitchen was cursing at each other until we ran out of chickens to fry.

When the last plate was served and the final curse

muttered under breath, I locked the front gate to the entrance. The metal groaned. My key turned with a reluctant click, and I exhaled, steam rising in the cold night air.

I stood there, eyelids heavy, the world swaying. A gust of wind carried the sour tang of spilled beer and car exhaust. Shaking the sleep from my head, I had one more stop to make before I could go home.

Nobody else was in the street. Not that could be seen at least. Something always lurked in the shadows. Most people never noticed the demons hiding in the dark corners, but since that night on the farm, I cannot ignore them.

Patting my pockets, I search for my phone, only to realize it was already in my hand. My other hand clutched a warm paper bag, grease soaking through the bottom. Inside: chopped barbecue sandwiches, pickles, fries, onion rings, and three slices of cheesecake.

I paid for all the food myself. Not because anyone would accuse me of stealing from work, but because it feels cleaner that way. Like I am buying penance.

Turning the corner, I saw Bob. He sat beneath a flickering streetlamp, its light stuttering. His K-9 companion, Pancake, lay curled beside him, its ribs visible beneath matted fur. The man hummed a soft sound. He often hummed happy songs because he was just one of those people who always had a sunny disposition about life, no matter what had befallen him in the past.

Every day, I found Bob sitting here on this curb, and sometimes with friends. Some nights, I could find them shelter, and a few times I even managed to get him some time to talk to one of the psychology professors at school. The man was too proud to ever ask for help and even turned me away on a couple of occasions, but that was a story for another time.

When he recognized me, his face lit up. The humming grew louder, almost manic. Pancake lifted his head, ears twitching.

The concrete was cold and damp beneath me as I sat beside him. "Where are Jane and Jimmy?" Ignoring the smell of unwashed clothes and sweat, I thought about how often I kept him and his friends from starvation.

"They went to get help," he said, eyes distant.

Bob took the bag. He pulled out a sandwich and offered it to Pancake, who devoured it with desperate gulps.

"I brought cheesecake as a bonus tonight. Share it with whoever needs it."

Bob nodded, tears cutting clean lines through the grime on his cheeks as he grabbed a sandwich for himself. "Thank you, Adam. You're always good to us."

We talked while he ate. About my grandma. About the farm. About things that felt safe, but the air around us felt wrong. It was too still, too quiet. A shadow moved behind a dumpster. Just the wind, maybe.

The conversation drifted on to the meaning of life and whether every person had a divine purpose.

He encouraged me to stick with school this time between his bites. "Everyone has some purpose, whether it's divine or just to exist, I don't really know. What I do know is sometimes fate is a cruel mistress."

The conversation shifted to lighter subjects, and Bob laughed at one of my stories, but it sounded forced. He would not let me find him a place to sleep for the night; he was always more of a challenge than Jana and Jimmy.

"You should find yourself a nice girl and settle down," he said.

I shook my head and stared at the pothole in front of us. "That's probably not a good idea. There are dangerous things that happen in my life. Bringing someone close to me would not be safe, or even possible."

Bob shook his head and patted me on the shoulder. "You are young. Whatever danger lurks out there, it's better faced when you have someone to back you up." He patted the old German shepherd snoring beside him with a full belly.

My bones ached as a yawned escaped my lips. "I should go. Find a friend or two tonight to share that food."

"I will, thank you, Adam," he replied, clutching the bag close to his chest.

"See you tomorrow, Bob."

Each step was heavier than the last as I walked away. The street stretched longer than it should. The lamps flickered. A dog barked in the distance. The rest of the short walk home felt like an entirely uphill climb.

Reaching my door, I unlocked it, slipped in, and locked both deadbolts. My bag dropped on the couch, and the keys clattered onto the table as I made my way to the bedroom. My room was dark, and the air was stale as I collapsed onto the bed, the springs in the mattress groaning beneath me.

"Booger," I muttered. "Need to set the alarm."

I fumbled for my phone, with one eye open, and set an alarm for 6:55 a.m. I slid it on the shelf in my headboard and made myself comfortable.

Outside, something scratched against the window. It was probably just a rat, and no reason to think otherwise tonight.

Sleep came swift and without warning. One breath, maybe two, and I was gone, but peace did not follow. My body jerked under the sheets as nightmares clawed their way into my mind.

A small girl named Nia sat on her bed in the darkness. She was pleading, her eyes bulged with terror, and somewhere above her, an Archangel descended with great, burning wings, its face veiled in light too bright to bear. The dream shifted, yanked sideways like a film reel skipping frames.

I floated... no, was pulled out of myself, rising into a sky that smelled of dust and blood. Below, a battlefield sprawled across the American plains: bison stampeded through smoke, totems were cracked and covered in blood. With bone-white claws, shapeshifters tore apart native warriors. The air was thick with war cries and the metallic sting of ozone as a tall, bearded man stepped through the smoke, wearing a star on his chest with one point missing.

As fast as the bloody nightmare ended, I was in my bed with eyes wide open, but my body refused to move.

A crushing weight pinned me to the mattress, pressing from scalp to soles that slowly consumed me. My chest burned. My limbs tingled. A hot breeze swirled around me, reeking of scorched feathers. My throat dried and my eyes stung.

Only a rasp escaped as I tried to scream. My muscles strained and trembled beneath the invisible force. I clenched my jaw, squeezed my eyes shut, and whispered through cracked lips, "In the name of Jesus Christ, I demand you to release me..."

The pressure vanished. My lungs flooded with stale, sour air as I gasped. My eyes stayed shut, but I sat up, swinging my sweat-soaked legs over the edge of the bed. I mumbled another quick prayer for good measure.

"Leave, for he is the light and the way, so I banish you with the power of his name, Jesus Christ. Whatever is not of the Lord, I bade you leave! Amen."

I sat for a moment, with my eyes closed, and

controlled my breathing till my heart stopped pounding.

With all the things that happened to me over the past few years, I had become paranoid that one day, that demon on Grandma's farm would claw its way out of hell again and find me.

"Shit," I muttered, wiping my brow. My fingers trembled as I reached for my phone, fumbling against the headboard until the screen lit with a pale blue glow. 2:59 a.m. Battery at 10%. "Crud," I hissed. "Forgot to plug it in again."

The light from the screen revealed a rectangular shape hovering about five feet above the bed. I squinted at a massive, chained door as the blue glow from my phone cast eerie shadows across its surface. The surface was iron, but it appeared to have been forged to resemble wood, with grain patterns twisted into snarling demonic faces. Maybe it was the light, but their mouths seemed to move gradually, deliberately, like they were tasting the air.

The smell of sewage and wet metal crawled into my nostrils, burned my sinuses, and coated my tongue with a bitter film. My skin prickled as if the stench itself had weight, pressing against me. My stomach was clenched, bile rising.

I rubbed my eyes with tears streaming from the horrible stench. This was hopefully another dream, but the door remained. No knob. No handle. Just three rusty hinges and a plaque etched with jagged letters: *PAIN*.

"What kind of shit is this now?" I muttered, breathing through my mouth, only to taste the rot. The flavor was like licking a corroded pipe dipped in spoiled meat.

Standing, legs shaky, as I reached. My fingers brushed the surface.

A chill surged up my arm. A sizzling sound followed, like flesh meeting dry ice. Electric and numbing pain exploded through my hand. My fingers spasmed, cramping inward. I staggered backward, nearly collapsing.

Frost spread across the door, creeping to the outer edges in jagged veins. The temperature dropped as if I had just stepped into a deep freezer. My breath fogged. Goosebumps erupted across my skin, and my joints ached with the sudden chill. The warmth drained from me as I pulled into the door.

I stared at my fingertips. Red blotches swelled, then blistered. "Lord," I whispered, "guide me to do what must be done." The raw marks turned white and throbbed.

The door shuddered. A low vibration hummed through the floorboards, through my bones. The barrier cracked open, just a sliver, and a blinding red light spilled out, flooding the room in a hellish glow. I shielded my eyes, blinking against the glare, and dropped to the floor to lace up my Vans.

Once they were on, I stood before the door and kicked at the demonic portal.

The moment my shoe touched the door, the rubber began to hiss and melt. Acrid smoke curled upward, stinging my nose and gagging me. The door resisted, heavy despite its suspension in the air. I kicked harder and forced it open about a foot.

White light burst forth, swirling around me. The strange sensation caressed my skin, lifted my hair, and tugged at my clothes. It was soft and staticky, and as quickly as it came, it vanished.

The smell returned worse than before. A tidal wave of rot and sulfur, of maggot-ridden meat and burning flesh, slammed into me, curling my stomach into knots. I doubled over, dry-heaving, throat raw and eyes watering. Bile dribbled from my mouth, splashing onto my shoes, burning like vinegar in a sore throat.

The red glimmer was an inconsistent strobe light, slow at first, then increasing in speed. My head spun. My knees buckled. I had fought demons before, but this... this was different. This was sickness. This was corruption made flesh.

In all my years of battling demons, I had never experienced anything like this. There was nothing to fight but the stench.

The white beam returned, soft and enveloping. My eyes closed. Peace settled over me. I opened them again and saw myself standing on a dirt road that stretched into nothing. A presence beyond the light beckoned me to come closer.

Each step forward felt like wading through molasses. The light grew brighter, wrapping around me as if cold hands reached through it, gripping my limbs. The darkness pressed in, refusing to yield to the light's strength.

It swallowed everything. From somewhere nearby, a voice whispered, "You are in the land of Un. Do not fear. You have another journey to take, and I will be with you."

The radiance pushed outward, revealing a barren wasteland with ashen trees clawing at the sky. The wind howled with the cries of abandoned children. The branches creaked. A sense of nothingness was here as the desert stretched as far as I could see, with only dead trees scattered throughout.

Far off, in the moonless desert, stood a child. Small. Still.

Somehow, I heard her voice, soft and clear, as if she were beside me: "He is waiting for you."

I shivered. My eyes opened, and I was still in bed, but the hovering demonic door was still in my apartment and opened wide.

The grotesque stench had vanished as if sucked into a

vacuum, leaving behind only the faint, familiar scent of my apartment: fabric softener, old wood, and the day-old fried food left sitting on the counter. However, my legs moved forward, unbidden. I neither commanded nor resisted them. Like a passenger in my own body, I was gliding toward the open door.

I stopped, not by choice. My feet locked in place, as if the floor had turned to glue. My breath caught. My heart froze mid-beat, and a wave of numbness surged through me.

I was no longer in New York. The new place resembled a room in shape alone; everything else defied the concept. It was a chamber of torment, a cathedral of suffering. The walls were not walls; they were stacked human bodies, twisted and nailed together like grotesque lumber. Naked men and women writhed, their flesh bubbling and sloughing off like wax. Black ichor oozed from their wounds, congealing into thick ropes that clung to their skin like tar.

Each body was impaled by a spike the size of a railroad tie, driven through torsos, necks, and limbs. Each body was methodical, stacked like cordwood, forming the walls and ceiling. It was an architecture of agony.

The floor was a lake of molten lava, but it radiated no heat. Instead, a warm, unsettlingly gentle breeze drifted across my skin. Floating atop the lava were slabs of ice. Slick, translucent, and intact as they formed a path. They were stepping stones in a garden built by a lunatic.

The air shimmered with a sickly red hue. Shadows danced across the melting bodies, their movements jerky and puppet-like, as if some unseen hand yanked their strings. Their heads twisted unnaturally, searching for any escape.

I leaned closer. The tortured mouths gaped wide, but

inside, there were no tongues or teeth to be seen. They were just hollow caverns filled with black sludge that shuddered with the rhythm of a diseased heart. Their moans were muffled under the ooze.

One figure near me, a woman, maybe, reached with a skeletal arm, her fingers melting mid-motion. The moan escaping her was softer, almost pleading. Her face was a ruin of melted skin and empty sockets, yet somehow, she still begged.

My heart ripped in half as all these poor souls suffered.

A sphere of liquid fire appeared, hovering near the wall, throbbing with malevolence. The orb drifted like a predator, daring the damned to scream. Those closest to it trembled violently, their bodies convulsing with such force that bones snapped as if they were dry twigs. Flesh peeled back, yet they remained silent, their agony swallowed by fear as it drifted towards the loudest moans.

The fireball weaved through the air like a serpent. When it neared one of the writhing bodies, the reaction was instant: spasms, fractures, and the wet sound of meat tearing. When one body was reduced to a pile of steaming clumps, another was pushed through the pile and impaled in its place, the cycle restarting as a never-ending machine.

"What kind of hell have I entered?" The fiery orb moved around the room, chasing the moans and cries of the damned, but did not approach me.

I shut my eyes and prayed for strength. For faith to hold against whatever this was. Whispering words of armor, I hoped they would shield me from the madness clawing at my sanity. Losing my faith was not an option, no matter what this demon world showed me. If this was a dream, it was time to wake up now.

When I opened my eyes, the horror had evolved into more.

Ahead of me hung a man suspended like a marionette, his limbs bound by ropes of intestines. They wrapped around his neck, wrists, waist, and ankles, taut and glistening. His head drooped forward, hair black as raven feathers, unmoving except when the warm breeze swayed him gently, carrying the putrid smell of sickly shit.

He was perhaps seven feet tall and lean, but his body was a canvas of torment. Gashes crisscrossed his skin, bruises bloomed the color of rotting fruit, and his back bristled with knives of every shape and size. Beneath him, white feathers lay scattered, each one ablaze with flames but never burned.

Beside him stood two demonic creatures, child-sized and repulsive. Their skin was a patchwork of grey rot, riddled with pus-filled blisters, and covered in congealed blood. Maggots wriggled in and out of their flesh, leaving trails of slime. They stood around the man, admiring their handiwork.

They began to whip him. The whips were tendrils of flame that slithered and snapped as if they were alive, striking his flesh with explosive force. Sometimes, even without the creature's arm swinging.

Each lash tore chunks of meat, revealing muscle and bone. The man did not scream. He did not flinch, but the demons laughed deep, guttural sounds. They skipped and hopped around the man as they danced like kids who had been given a new toy.

My head spun. The air thickened, pressing against my skull. I tried to anchor myself, to focus and breathe, but the room resonated with suffering, and my senses began to blur. A little prayer in my head was all I could manage for this blasphemous dream to end.

The fireball slowed. The demons paused, their laughter cut short. They appeared confused as they sniffed the air with animalistic snorts and grunts. Even I felt that the presence in the room had changed.

Their eyes, if you could call those pits eyes, locked onto me. Their bodies stiffened and their backs straightened.

At that moment, I knew. I was not supposed to be here. The creatures had discovered an intruder in their house, and they were deciding what to do with me.

My heart thundered against my ribs, each heartbeat a violent drumroll that threatened to rupture my chest. The two creatures had turned toward me now, their malformed faces bathed in the hellish red glow that bled from the walls. I tried to look away, but my gaze was shackled to theirs. Our eyes were locked in a grotesque communion.

Their faces were a mockery of beauty. Each had two eyes, but one bulged grotesquely, milky and veined, while the other shrank into a socket too deep to see. Where a nose should be, there was only a gaping hole, rimmed with dried and flaky flesh. Their mouths peeled open, crowded with jagged, yellow teeth that jutted from the gums like cracked tombstones, too many for their jaws to contain. Black saliva dribbled down their chins, bubbling and hissing as it hit the scorched floor.

My unblinking eyes began to burn, as if I were staring into a furnace. The air shimmered with heat, but my skin felt only a warm breeze.

I shut my eyes and whispered to myself, "If this is a dream, let me wake."

A voice came, not through my ears, but inside my skull, like a thought not my own.

"You should not be here," it said, weary and frayed. "Turn around. Close the door. I can only protect you for a little longer."

The tone was sorrowful. In my head, I answered, "Who are you? What is this place? Am I dreaming?"

"No," the speaker replied, trembling with anguish. "This is real. I do not know how you arrived. Now go!"

Despite the pain and anguish in the words, it was still potent, and my brain vibrated with every syllable. I could not leave this person here.

"What can I do to help? What is your name?"

"I do not have a name. I am paying for my sin, and you are interrupting the ritual. I'm the reason you have not been reduced to ashes. You must leave before my love for you fails."

Something was familiar about the speaker. So, I pressed harder. "Are you the one who helped me defeat the dark figure?"

"Yes," the voice whispered.

My eyes opened just as the hanging man raised his arm, palm outstretched. A gust of calm, clean, and gentle wind swept me backward through the door and onto my bed with a thud that rattled the frame.

The door began to close, fading into a cloud of smoke. Desperate, I tore the pillowcase from my pillow and lunged, wrapping the fabric around one of the chains. The metal was freezing, biting into my skin, but I held fast. The door shimmered before fading, and I, along with it. On the other side was a dark hallway lined with doors.

My hand was numb and aching as I released the door. The fabric clung to the chain like a flag. My childhood pillowcase fluttered as the chain wrapped tighter around the door, offering me a glimpse of a circular black ear. "Thank you, Mickey Mouse," I muttered.

Gripping the door, I pulled and ignored the searing cold and blistering heat that surged through my palms. The metal groaned, resisting, but I dug deeper into myself, pulling with everything I had.

All I wanted was to repay the kindness of those who

had helped me. The door began to give way as I dug deeper into my soul, praying silently for the strength I needed.

The door opened, just enough to squeeze through, finding myself once again in the chamber of torments. The demons were still there, their whips of living flame lashing the man's broken body. The moment I stepped inside, they turned, their heads snapping toward me with unnatural speed.

Fueled by rage and desperation, I charged them.

Before I could reach them, the voice rang out, thunderously booming through the wailing chamber. "How did you find your way here?! I told you to leave!"

"I won't abandon you!" I shouted. "You helped me. I'll help you! I'll fight these ugly ass demons!"

"You should not be here," the voice replied, heavy with sorrow. "I must pay for my sins. Your efforts are wasted. I do not deserve help. Leave!"

"Then I'll die doing what's right!"

The demons lunged, grotesque smiles splitting their faces. Their mouths frothed with black sludge, thick and bubbling, dripping onto the floor with a hiss. They spun their flaming whips like deranged lion tamers, the fire shrieking as it sliced through the air.

I touched my ring. A sword materialized in my hand, its blade humming with divine energy. The holy blade had not been drawn in months, and it was good to feel its weight in my hand again. This was my purpose, this was why I was alone. No demon would cause harm to anyone as long as the sword answered my summons.

An authoritative voice filled the room, and the wails from the walls and ceiling fell silent. "No! No harm shall befall him. I will not allow it."

An invisible force held me back. My muscles were screaming as I strained, but I could not advance. The demons froze, too, snarling and snapping. Their frustration boiled over, and they turned on each other, growling and clawing at one another.

They stopped, turned toward the man still hanging in the center of the room, and began to growl. He had not moved. His body was limp, arms raised, wounds bleeding.

The ropes, those grotesque cords of intestine, fell away. The man tilted until he was upright, as if unseen hands had held him. His feet touched the ground, and he approached us.

The demons shrieked, high-pitched piglike squeals as he drew closer to them. They retreated, trembling, their whips extinguished and fell to the ground. The man's presence was a tide washing over them, and they were being swept up in it.

He raised his hand. The air cracked, and their faces imploded as if struck by an invisible force. Black sludge erupted from their mouths, splattering the walls. Their bodies convulsed and collapsed inward. The chamber echoed with the wet, sickening sound of their destruction.

The demons collapsed in a wet heap of shredded flesh. Their bones shattered, their twisted forms twitching once before rising, levitating two feet off the scorched ground. They drifted toward the molten lake, tumbling through the air. The fire accepted them, swallowing their remains with a gurgle of flames.

The man approached across the cracked obsidian floor on bare feet. When his hand touched my shoulder, a wave of warmth surged through me. My sword dissolved, collapsing into a shimmer of light that coiled onto my finger with a faint metallic ringing.

I looked at him. He smiled a quiet, weary smile, and I returned it, though my heart still trembled.

Around him, white dust began to swirl, rising from the ground. As it touched his torn skin, the wounds closed, leaving behind smooth, glowing flesh that radiated a faint, divine warmth. A robe of pure white unfurled from his shoulders, wrapping him in cloth that seemed woven from a pale light, falling to his knees in gentle folds.

The angelic plumes followed with a deep, thunderous flutter. Two enormous ivory wings erupted from the man's back, feathers unfurling with a rush of displaced air. They stretched wide, casting long shadows across the chamber. He flexed them cautiously, testing their strength, each movement stirring the dust around us into spiraling halos.

The wings spanned close to sixteen feet, their tips brushing the edges of the chamber. They glowed faintly, veins of gold threading through the feathers. As the tips drifted near the bodies in the walls, the squirming forms seemed to calm momentarily.

"Thank you for trying to save me, but I didn't need saving. They couldn't truly harm me. I allowed them to mark my flesh... because I deserved it."

I blinked, confused. "What?"

His eyes dimmed. He lowered his head. "I let them punish me for my sin. I am an Archangel. I disobeyed."

The air was thick with the sharp odor of scorched stone. "What did you do?"

He met my gaze, and the weight of eternity seemed to press behind his eyes. "I helped you."

"You wanted them to do this to you... because you helped me?" My voice cracked. "You let them cut you, burn you, torture you, knowing you could stop it whenever you wanted?"

He nodded. "Yes, but you don't understand. I was forbidden to interfere. I prayed for permission. I was denied."

I stepped back, the ground beneath me slick with sticky ichor from the demons he had squashed. "Who told you not to help me? Why?"

"Do not dwell on what's already paid," he said. "I questioned my orders. I refused to allow you to die. I cast aside prayers and chose action. I borrowed a feather from a friend's wing and sent it to Earth to find you. I would not let you die at the hands of that demon. It was to be your fate, but I would not stand by, and so I announced my resistance to the heavens."

I retreated, with my hand hovering over my ring. "Are you... a demon now?"

He smiled, the light around him softening. "No. I am still an Angel, an archangel who loved humanity more than I was allowed. I watched you praying to our father in a time of need. Instead of giving in to father's will, I took matters into my own hands."

"But didn't you rebel? How are you not a demon like the other rebel angels?"

"Not like the others," he said. "They wanted Heaven for themselves. They hated humans for being loved by our father more than they were. He told them he had enough love for both the divine and humanity, but in their vanity and pride, they could not accept their role as protectors and wanted humanity to be destroyed. I fought to protect you. I see humanity as children. You are flawed and fragile, but worthy."

"But you went against God."

"Yes... and no." He stepped closer, wings folding behind him. "Some angels are assigned at birth to guard a soul. We shield you from evil, but not from nature like earthquakes, aging, and fire. Unless given permission, we cannot interfere. Even though we are not as perfect as our father, and sometimes a soul is lost to the rebellious ones."

"Do you know who my guardian is?"

His smile faded, and his face was unreadable. "I am."

"You're the one who gave me the sword? The same one who helped me fight the dark figure?"

He nodded. "The sword belonged to an Archangel named Guardian. I asked her for a feather from one of her wings. Her feathers are powerful weapons against evil. She was one of the fiercest warriors that served under Michael."

"But you protected me like a guardian should, even though God said I should die."

"I wasn't supposed to, but I couldn't watch you die at the hands of that demon that had cursed your family for so long. I am not ordinary. I am an archangel. We are assigned to humans only for extraordinary reasons. I don't know what Father's plan is for you, but I knew it wasn't death."

"So... God wanted me dead?"

His expression hardened. "No. Our Father does not wish the end of life. He calls you home when it is time. What happens between birth and death is yours to shape. He gives you tools. He rejoices when you use them well. When a soul arrives before its time, Heaven mourns. I was wrong to ignore Father's plan. I was not ready for you to leave this world, and I intervened. In doing so, I have disrupted a bigger fate, and for that I surrendered myself to punishment."

The air was thick with incense and ash. "So, you let yourself be punished... because you disobeyed?"

"Yes. We hold ourselves to standards of loyalty and grace. I have commanded legions. I must be held accountable for my disobedience."

"Why didn't you punish yourself?"

"We do not harm ourselves. That would be sin, but we accept punishment as we see fit."

My mind was spinning, the chamber flickering with flame and the renewed wails. Was this real? A dream? A vision?

He must have sensed my confusion. "Do you trust me?"

"Yes," I whispered. "But I don't understand. I don't want to go back yet. I need answers."

"Not now," he said. "Close your eyes. Pray. When you wake, you'll be home."

"I don't want to go. I want answers. What bigger fate are you talking about?"

He smiled, patient and kind. There was a moment of hesitation before I closed my eyes. There was no point in pushing him further. There would be no answers today.

Weight vanished from my feet. My body lifted, floating upward like a leaf in a warm updraft. The air wrapped around me. My eyes remained closed, and I did not know if I could even open them.

As my prayer ended, I felt the floor beneath my feet.

My eyes opened, and I was in my room.

The door was gone. The archangel. The demons. The chamber of torment. All vanished.

Had I not faced demons before, I would have died from the shock of last night, but my family's legacy, our battles and scars, had prepared me. My faith held me together despite all the living nightmares I experienced.

Still, the horrors linger. I learned to block them when I must. To survive. To move forward.

Hunched on the edge of my bed, the sheets were cool against my skin. I lay back, letting the silence settle over.

The prayer formed on my lips so the rest of the night would be restful as I waited for sleep to come.

The next thing I knew, sunlight was slipping through the blinds. It flooded the room with a brightness that felt too clean and pure. My eyes recoiled from it, and I groaned, stretching my stiff limbs. My body felt embalmed in exhaustion, as if I had been buried alive and just clawed my way to the surface.

The bed beneath me radiated warmth, its mattress cradling me with deceptive softness. I peeled myself away and stumbled toward the dresser. The carpet was cool and gritty beneath my bare feet.

In the shower, the water hit me with a barrage of hot needles against chilled skin. Steam curled around me, thick and fragrant with the scent of soap. I rubbed my temples, trying to scrub away the memory of last night.

"Was it a dream?" I muttered aloud, voice muffled by the shower. "Did I really meet my guardian Angel? Why had he not been allowed to help me?"

A splash of moisture shot into my ear, and I jerked my head as a sharp ache grew behind my eyes. A dull but persistent headache formed. I tried to focus on the rhythm of the droplets against the tile, the plastic curtain swaying as my elbow brushed against it, and the faint, mildewy smell clinging to the grout. Something had to distract me from the ache, but the images from the night before clawed their way into my mind.

After drying off and dressing, I found myself in the living room, spooning cornflakes into my mouth as I went through my morning routine. The cereal was bland, and the milk was lukewarm. The cartoons flickered with manic colors and shrill voices that grated on my nerves.

23

I was on my second bowl, brain numbing with each laugh track, when I glanced at my phone. The screen was dim, and the battery icon was flashing red.

The chaos of "Spoons" filled the room until 8:30 a.m., trying to drown out the lingering dread from last night and those words about disrupting a bigger fate. My first class was at 9:30, and the day ahead stretched long and heavy, as my final class would not end until 3:30. It would only get worse. A late shift at the pub from 5 to 10, followed by a chapter meeting at 11 tonight with the fraternity. It would be a long night.

With a coffee on the way to campus, the bitter scent heightened my senses before I took my first sip. Through every lecture, hallway, and scribbled notes, my mind drifted. The nightmare played on repeat. The door. The demons. The twisted chamber of flesh and fire. My guardian's torment for not letting me die. I should be dead. Was that why I have been feeling so lost lately? Was I meant to be already gone?

By the time classes ended, I was dragging. My legs felt like sandbags, my thoughts filled with static. I walked toward work as the sky dimmed into twilight, and the air was thick with the scent of car exhaust and rot from the piles of garbage bags.

I heard the voice come from behind me.

"Adam, I need your help."

The voice was soft and unfamiliar, yet it struck me. I stumbled, heart lurching, and spun.

A child stood beneath the flickering streetlight, his silhouette small and still. He looked as if he had stepped out of a Dickens novel. He had dark eyes, too deep for his age, and thick curls shadowing a serene face. His clothes were loose, threadbare, and faded. The light behind him cast a halo of gold around his form.

"Who are you?" I asked, trying to keep my voice light.

"I do not have a name," he said, his voice flat, emotionless.

The air was suddenly dry as I cleared my throat. "Little one, I thought you were going to rob me or something worse. Aren't you too young to be walking alone?"

He stared at me, and his steady gaze made my skin crawl. "Adam, I need you to be quiet and listen."

I laughed nervously. "Is this a prank? Did Alba put you up to this? That John is always messing with people when they least expect it."

The child's expression did not change, but the way he looked at me made me feel small. "I do not have much time. I know who you are. Your guardian said you can help me."

The noise of the street vanished. No cars. No wind. No distant chatter. Just deafening silence.

The kid smiled, and the air around him shimmered. "Do not be afraid. I am an Angel. I need your help to save a mother and her unborn daughter. If you succeed, I will be the child's guardian. However, they are in danger right now. A demon is plaguing them as it is trying to possess the child's soul. It is driving the mother mad. If it succeeds, the child will become a force of destruction unlike anything Earth has ever known."

I swallowed hard. "Will you be helping me?"

The Angel lowered his head. "No."

The word hung in the air.

"I'll do my best," I said. "Can I ask you something personal?"

"Yes."

"Why don't Angels have names?"

"We do," he said. "If we are given one."

"Then why don't you or my guardian have one?"

"Did you give him one?"

"You mean... I'm supposed to?"

He nodded. "Guardians are named by those they protect, if the protected ever realizes they're being watched over. The name lives as long as the soul does. Sometimes, names are given by higher authorities when an Angel needs to be remembered, such as Gabriel and Michael, but most come from the bond."

The streetlight flickered above us. "Then I'll call my guardian... Knox."

The Angel paused, his gaze distant, as if listening beyond the veil of sound. He said. "Knox is pleased with that. Now, I need you to be ready for what must be done."

"How do you know he's happy with it?"

"He said so." His eyes gleamed. "Ask him yourself."

He gestured behind me, and as I turned, the temperature dropped. Knox stood there. His face was hard, but not cruel. It was a hardness born from centuries of grief.

"I am satisfied with Knox," he said, "but now you must understand what you're about to hear. What happens next... will determine whether the mother and child live past tomorrow."

The air around us remained still, as if the world itself was holding its breath.

"We are forbidden to help you," Knox continued. "Not in any action can we step in. Only in words are we allowed. Your sword may falter against this evil, and if you use it recklessly, you may kill the mother... and the baby she carries. A dead youth is easily possessed. There is no soul to resist. The death of the child would mean we failed to stop the demon from entering the world."

"What do I need to do?"

Knox's expression made deeper lines in his face. "You must face a demon... one who was once my closest friend."

The air chilled, and Adam watched his breath puff from his mouth.

"She was radiant once," he said, eyes glistening. "But she turned on Father. Took up weapons of hate against the Word. I fought her for a thousand years, and when I finally cast her down, I wept. I still do."

A single tear traced the curve of his cheek, glowing before vanishing into his skin.

"I never understood her rage," he whispered. "Perhaps she loved Father too much. Perhaps she could not bear to share Him with beings she deemed lesser. I was called to serve as a Guardian. I accepted without question, but had I not been summoned... I might still be lost in mourning."

The streets and buildings around were silent as if the stone itself listened to the archangel.

"She is cast out from Heaven," Knox said, "but not from our Father's heart. Nor mine. Her name is Zar. She wants revenge for my refusal to join her. She knows you are my ward. She will come for you if she frees herself."

Nodding with his sorrow, pressing against my chest. "I understand. I'll do whatever it takes."

Knox's eyes narrowed. "You must. If you fail, she will possess the mother and the child, and many more will suffer. She is not like any demon you have faced before. The dark figure was merely a pawn for her to reach out to you. She has been whispering to you from her prison for your entire life."

The other Angel stood waiting with calmness before a storm. I recalled the whispers calling my name. They had stopped after I defeated the dark figure. Had this Zar been the voice I heard on the bus that day when I returned to Grandma's farm?

"I need you to listen," Knox said. "If you do not, Zar will enter this world. Do you understand, Adam?"

27

"Yes, please continue. I will do whatever is necessary. What do I have to do?"

"You will enter the Between," he said. "A realm between realms. Someone will find you there. They will lead you to the Door of Suffering. Once you cross it, you are alone."

I frowned. "Why can't either of you take me there? Aren't you both Angels?"

They spoke in unison, their voices overlapping. "We are forbidden. No Angel or Archangel may interfere with the mother or child. Their fate lies in your hands... and her faith."

"But isn't this interference?"

Knox smiled, the corners of his mouth lifting with a trace of mischief. "We were told not to interfere with mother or child. You are not them. We are helping you understand. What you do with that knowledge... is yours alone."

Chuckling, despite the tension, I said, "You two are sneaky Angels."

Their smiles mirrored mine.

I turned to the nameless Angel. "Even though I'm not your ward... I want to give you a name. Jacob. It's from a book I love."

He blinked with a slow nod. "Jacob... Jacob. I like it. I will wear it until I am given another. Thank you."

The air hummed with unseen energy as I stood between the angels. "What do I do next?"

Jacob gestured to the ground. "Sit."

I lowered myself onto the cold sidewalk.

Knox stepped behind me. "Fear not."

His hands came over my eyes. They were warm and firm. The world vanished into darkness.

"We will now pray the Our Father," he said, voice close to my ear. "For your safety."

Jacob added, "When you open your eyes, you will be in the Between. There, you will find your guide."

The words of my prayer came slow, each syllable clearly enunciated through years of practiced repetition. The air around me was heavier, and the city's smells changed to something that reminded me of overcooked caramel and nuts. My hair on my arms stood on end.

When the final word left my lips, Knox's hands lifted, and my eyes opened.

A small girl knelt before me, her hands just pulling from my face. Her skin was pale, her eyes filled with sorrow. Behind her, the world shimmered gray, endless, and silent.

The girl's face was bathed in a soft, spectral glow. Her skin was porcelain tinged with a faint blue hue. Dark hair cascaded over her shoulders in gentle waves, the strands catching the ambient light. When she spoke, her voice was barely louder than a breath, yet it resonated through me like a bell struck in a cathedral.

"Hello, Adam," she said. "I've been waiting for you."

The girl's hands had been over my eyes, but I had not felt the shift from Knox's touch to hers. There had been no change in warmth, no movement, just her serene and still sudden presence.

I leaned back to take in the space around us. The only sound was the air humming with unrecognized energy. A soft blue light enveloped me, casting a gentle glow across my skin. Above my head, a sphere of pale light hovered. Staring at it did not hurt my eyes as expected. Its glow was soothing, like the warmth of a long-forgotten, yet cherished memory that had just been recalled.

All around us, men, women, and children sat in rows. Each was cloaked in the same blue hue and sat motionless, their hollow eyes pointed in the same direction. Their expressions were filled with sorrow, their bodies still as statues. The silence was oppressive, broken only by the faint sound of my breath.

My face scrunched in a grimace as I turned to the woman. She offered a gentle smile.

"Do not fear," she said. "You are safe here. This is the Between. A place where souls wait for justice. They were wronged in life, their bodies desecrated, their deaths unanswered. They wait to witness the judgment of those who stole their peace."

"I hope this isn't rude," I said, voice trembling. "But... who are you?"

"I am not offended," she replied. "I am the guardian of this place, and the Archangel whose sword you've wielded. My name is Guardian. That is my duty."

She rose, her form shifting as she stood. The soft gown she wore dissolved into radiant armor, its plates of chromed steel shimmering with a warm, golden light. Her height doubled, towering above me, yet her presence remained gentle.

Around us, the silence broke as soft giggles and clapping echoed, as if children were playing and dancing in the rain on a hot summer day. The sound was hauntingly beautiful, and for a moment, I found myself smiling.

"So you're the Archangel Knox spoke of?" I asked.

She nodded, her expression proud. "Yes. Does the sword serve you well?"

"It does," I said. "I've used it to strike down every demon I've faced."

Her smile deepened before I asked, "Will you be taking me to the door?"

One tear rolled down her cheek, reflecting the blueish light of the orb above me. She wiped it quickly, but the sadness lingered.

"No," she said. "I cannot take you to the door. If I

lead you, it will not appear."

"Why are you crying? I didn't mean to upset you. I was told to ask the first person I met."

"I am not a person," she said. "I am an Archangel, but the child behind you is… and she will take you. She is one of my wards."

A small, warm, soft hand slipped into mine. A little girl, no taller than my hip, with plump, baby-fat cheeks and straight, red hair, stood beside me. Her blue eyes shimmered, and her smile was gentle. My breath caught. She was beautiful, and she was dead.

The realization hit me like a blow to the chest. The girl had passed into this place, murdered, and was now waiting for justice. A lump formed in my throat, and I knelt before her, wrapping her in a trembling embrace. Tears spilled freely, hot and bitter.

"My name is Daisy," she whispered. "Please don't cry for me. I'm in a better place now. Soon, I'll journey into the next world, where love is the only thing that exists. Cry for those who still suffer and live."

She let go of my hand and brushed my tears with a featherlight touch. Cupping my face, she squeezed.

"Give me your hand," she said. "Walk with me. We're going to save an innocent life that hasn't yet begun."

Standing with a heart aching, I nodded.

A finger pointed into a darkness so vast that it seemed to consume light. "We must go far from Guardian's protection. That is where the door waits."

I squinted, trying to pierce the void, but saw nothing, only blackness.

Noticing my hesitation. "We're going to find the door in the darkness. It's where sadness lives."

She pointed again, this time in a different direction. I looked at her, and she met my gaze with confidence.

"Just trust me."

"After you."

"No," she said. "Together, but I will not return. My journey ends there."

We stepped forward.

On the first step, a soft light illuminated around us, casting long shadows that flickered. "What do you mean?"

"I must remain behind," she said.

On the second step, tears welled in my eyes, blurring the edges of the path.

On the third step, she smiled. "Don't worry. This is how it must be."

On the fourth step, my tears spilled over, creating warm, salty trails on my cheeks. Each one was a silent scream from my soul.

On the fifth step, I stopped. "I can't let you sacrifice yourself. I won't go further unless there's another way to find the door."

She paused, her hand was still in mine. "If that's what you want... then we need not go further. We are already where we need to be."

Two feet away, suspended in the void, hung the door.

It hovered in midair, nailed to nothing, surrounded by the shadows. Its surface was dark, almost wet-looking, and the air around it smelled of rust. I stared, expecting it to burst open and release the demons that dwelled behind it.

"How?" I whispered. "How did we get here with only a few steps?"

Daisy looked at me, her voice soft and sad. "Distance means nothing here, only love for God our Father. Don't try to understand how. Just remember why."

The outline of the door was wavering like a heat mirage. The solidity of it refused to settle into focus. Without warning, a rush of hot, sticky air burst from its seams, coating my skin in a film of damp heat.

A red glow pulsed from within the door's surface. It was slow at first, but it grew stronger and faster. The hue deepened into a deep crimson, casting flickering shadows across the ground. The door itself began to ripple, its surface rippling as a bedsheet seized in a storm wind, flapping against invisible currents.

A faint moan sounded from the door as if it cried in pain. Paint peeled in brittle flakes, drifting into the air. The moan grew louder, more anguished, until it sounded more like a chorus of suffering trapped behind the grain. I stepped closer to get a better look at the door. Etched deep into the center, the word *SUFFERING was* carved with messy strokes that bled.

My breath was shallow, and my heart was hammering. Daisy's voice came to me, soft and steady: "Go ahead and open it. It cannot hurt you. I promise."

I reached for the red glowing doorknob, bracing myself for the heat, the pain, and the hiss of flesh. My fingers hovered, trembling. I touched it.

Instead of fire, a brutal cold surged up my arm, as if I plunged my bare hand into a bucket of ice water. The metal was slick, almost oily, and the chill crept into my bones, raising goose bumps across my skin.

Squeezing Daisy's hand. "Ouch," she whispered.

I released the knob and stepped back. "Sorry, Daisy, I didn't mean to…"

The door moved on its own.

The barrier creaked open inch by inch, groaning. Wet sobs, grinding wood, distant screams. With each bit it opened, it cried louder, as if a wound were tearing wider.

The portal stood open. Beyond the threshold was nothing. No light. No shape. Just a void so absolute it swallowed the glow around us. Even the soft blue light that had followed us dimmed, unable to penetrate the blackness.

The darkness shimmered, deep red veins swirling like blood in water. It thrummed, slow and deliberate, as if it were a predator breathing in the shadows. I stared into it and felt a presence stare back.

Hatred poured from the void, suffocating and ancient. It pressed against my chest, my lungs ached, and my throat tightened. I staggered, gasping, but my eyes refused to look away. I was snared.

The voice came in a slow, melodic tone.

"It will be okay if you enter. We do not hide. Just close your eyes and rest in our arms for the night. We will keep you from the light."

The sound was soft. Soothing. Almost maternal, but beneath the lullaby was hunger. The voice repeated the lyrics, each time smoother, sweeter, more seductive.

"Come inside. Rest. Let go. We will keep you safe from the light."

My body swayed. My mind dulled as the words wrapped around me. I felt myself leaning forward, drawn to the promise of peace, of sleep, of surrender from all the pain of living.

"It will be okay. Close your eyes and surrender into our arms. Rest."

A small hand, warm and trembling, squeezed mine.

"Adam," Daisy whispered. "Please... look at me."

My head turned, but my eyes remained locked on the swirling void. The voice grew louder, more insistent.

"Come on in. Everything will be okay. Reach out to me."

"Adam!" Daisy broke through the haze. "Look at me before it's too late!"

The thunderous words echoed in my skull, rattling my teeth, snapping the trance.

She grinned, but her eyes were fierce. "I said, listen to

me."

The disembodied whisper vanished. Silence rushed in as my mind reeled. My legs wobbled as I turned my back on the door. Daisy's lips moved, but her words were muffled. I stumbled, mind fogged, with instincts screaming to escape.

My only desire was to run. To flee. To escape the thing that had tried to claim me, but my body did not respond. I fall slowly, as if I were a puppet cut from its strings. I snapped into myself as if I had been struck by lightning.

From the ground, I was breathing in bursts, my heart pounding. Above me, Daisy's eyes, clear, kind, and full of worry, stared into mine.

Her lips moved, but at first, her voice was lost in the haze swirling through my head. Like a radio tuning through interference, I heard her, soft and urgent.

"… Okay? Are you okay?"

I blinked at Daisy, her pale face framed by the dim and unnatural glow that still lingered around us. My limbs felt heavy, and my chest felt hollow. "Yes," I said. "Just… lightheaded. What happened?"

"You started walking into the void," she said. "I had to scream and pull you back. If I hadn't, you would've crossed before me, and you wouldn't have come back."

The air around the door still hummed. I did not dare look at it again directly. Even now, I could hear the syrupy, sweet singing from the dark.

"Come to me, my child…"

My voice is barely a whisper. "What can we do against something I can't even look at?"

She met my gaze, her eyes steady. "Let me do what I came here to do."

My stomach dropped. "What do you mean?" I asked, though I already knew.

Her expression hardened, but her tone remained

gentle. "I must enter first. Let myself be taken. My innocence will wound it. A soul like mine... it can't digest. My innocence will weaken it."

I swallowed hard. "What do I need to do?"

A single tear slid down her cheek. "Stand up. Close your eyes. Count to five. Then take three steps at the door. Keep your eyes shut until you hear a water drop. That sound will be your signal, but be ready because my purity may be used against you. Once I enter, you'll be alone."

I nodded, throat tight, tears making trails on my face. Even after releasing the girl's hand, the warmth of her palm lingered.

She walked to the door, each step echoing louder than it should. Just inches from the threshold, she turned and smiled.

I stood and faced the door as I closed my eyes. The air grew colder, heavier. I counted to five and stepped forward.

One step.

Two steps.

Three.

At that moment, I stopped to wait for the sound of a water drop.

Screams tore through the air. They came from everywhere and nowhere, bouncing off invisible walls, vibrating through my bones. My skin crawled, my joints ached, and my stomach twisted as if poisoned. My eyes clenched shut, fighting the urge to flee.

The touches came. Cold. So cold they burned. Like ice needles driven into my flesh, each one a kiss of agony. My muscles locked, my breath caught. What touched me was savoring it, feeding on my pain.

Tears streamed down my face, and just as I thought I would collapse, I heard it.

A single water drop. Clear. Sharp. As loud as a bell tolling in the dead of night.

The sword was in my hand in an instant as I opened my eyes.

A pristine living room replaced the void. The space was bright, sterile, and calm. Plush couches, a gleaming mahogany coffee table, and sleek technology surrounded me. The air smelled of lavender and lemon polish. Too clean. Too perfect.

Sword in hand, I spun, expecting an ambush, but nothing moved. No shadows. No whispers. Just silence. The room was as if no children or pets had ever lived here.

My head spun, the world tilting like a carousel. The motion sickness made me feel five years old again as I battled the dizziness and nausea, seconds from vomiting.

There were three knocks. The knocks were clearly audible, but neither loud nor threatening. There were three more. Followed by a sweet voice, almost cheerful.

"Hello? Anybody there?"

Gritting my teeth. "Come on in," I growled. "I'm ready for you."

The doorknob twitched. I lifted the sword and waited for the demon to enter.

Metal scraped against metal somewhere in the mechanism of the doorknob, a high-pitched squeal that made my spine stiffen. The handle turned at a snail's pace, resisting and groaning as if it did not want to obey.

It stopped. A soft voice, almost apologetic, drifted through the door.

"I'll come back later if you don't want me to clean right now."

That sounded more like a hotel maid than a demon. It made no sense.

"I'll come back later..."

The words echoed strangely. The knob went still. This made no sense. Where am I?

My body tensed as the lock jiggled again.

A sonorous gong rang from an old grandfather clock. A glance around the room revealed no such furniture here.

My heart pounded, fast and hard. Chills ran up my spine as I tried to ignore the loud noise that had to be in my head somehow. I focused on the door and waited for the demon to enter this time.

Gong! Sweat beaded across my skin, soaking through my shirt.

Gong! Whoever was behind that door was enjoying this.

Gong! The lock clicked as if someone had turned a key.

Gong! The knob was still again. I recalled the words Daisy had said to me. "Let me do what I came here to do."

Gong! The door moved slowly, as if someone had leaned into it.

Gong! Silence.

Gong! A scraping sound of a nail from the other side of the door.

Gong! The hinges groaned, resisting, then gave way.

Gong! The door creaked open halfway.

Gong! I snarled, voice low and venomous. "Come on, Zar. Face me, you piece of garbage."

Gong! I lunged forward, sword raised, ready to strike, but I froze as a woman stepped through the door.

She stood beneath the sterile glow of recessed lighting, keys clinking in her right hand as she zipped her purse with her left. The movements were brisk and mundane, much like those of a human. She did not see me. Not until I stopped, sword steady, the blade inches from her throat.

The scream that tore through the room was shrill, and so loud it made my ears ring. Her purse and keys flew into the air, clattering against the hardwood floor. The demon collapsed, limbs folding beneath her, trembling as she curled into herself.

The thing shielded her face, bracing for a blow that never came.

"What's going on, demon?" I barked.

She looked up, eyes wide, pupils dilated, and her breath came in shallow gasps. Her gaze locked onto mine, searching for mercy, maybe. Or recognition. Whatever she saw made her eyes roll back, and she crumpled, limp and silent.

The sword was gripped so tightly my knuckles burned. My fingers had gone numb, and the anticipation of battle coiled in my muscles. I should have struck while I had the advantage, but something about her did not feel right.

Circling her, and glancing to the open door behind her, I half-expect claws or fire to burst through. Nothing came; it was just an empty hallway, as in any high-rise apartment building. I closed the door and locked it with a soft click.

I turned my full attention to the woman on the floor.

She lay on her side, chest rising and falling in shallow, erratic breaths. I nudged her onto her back with the toe of my boot, sword still poised. The flesh was warm to the touch. The devilish fiend looked human.

Long, inky dark waves of hair spilled across the floor. The woman's skin was sun-kissed, smooth, and flushed. She wore a tailored, charcoal-gray business suit, crisp and expensive. The heels had come off in the fall, revealing bare feet with chipped nail polish. The demon had taken the form of a tall and elegant woman in her early thirties.

"If you weren't a demon, I would think you were

gorgeous."

The blade pressed to her throat, the edge cold against her neck. My foot nudged her, and her eyes fluttered open. She screamed again for a second but did not move. One twitch, and her blood would paint the floor.

"Please!" she sobbed. "Please, don't kill me. You can take my money. There's two hundred in my purse, and fifty more in change on the dresser. I won't call the cops, I swear. Just... please don't kill me!"

Her voice cracked as I withdrew, confused. Was this a trick? A demon's ploy? Her tears were real. She crawled to her knees, hands trembling and body shaking.

"If y-you want something else," she stammered, "just... please, make it quick."

Narrowing my eyes. "Unholy one, what do you mean? Robbery? Something else?"

Tears streaked her cheeks. "Aren't you here to rob me? Or... or..." Her voice faltered. "Then... why... why are you here?"

My sword lowered, but was still ready. "Me? What about you, demon? You look like a woman. Business clothes, a clean apartment. You ask me why I'm here. Where's the hellfire? The lake of boiling bodies? Are you not Zar?"

Her eyes widened, lips trembling, as she covered her mouth to whisper, "No... I'm not Zar. I'm Bell. My name is Bell. I live here. I'm not a demon."

She paused for a second, "Zar... she holds my soul. I made a deal."

Her body shook with sobs, the kind that wrack the spine and leave the lungs gasping. I had never seen anyone cry as if their soul was trying to escape through their tears.

"If you're not the hell spawn I seek, then why did the door bring me here?"

Wiping her face, she steadied her breath. "This isn't hell. This is my apartment. In New York City."

The words hit me like a brick, the room spun, and the clean scent of lavender overwhelmed me. "If that's true, then why did the Door of Sorrow bring me back to the city I was already in? I'm not supposed to be here."

She froze. Her eyes widened. "You came through a door?"

"Yes," I said. "Do you know it?"

She shook her head. "Not that door, but I know one called Regret. I walked through it once." Her eyes stared off as if she was seeing her past unfold in front of her. "It took everything."

With her hands dropped to her lap, her gaze fell to the floor between us, as if the answer lay in the grain of the wood.

The words struck me, and I stepped closer, prepared for any trick. "Before I decide what to do with you, you have one chance. Convince me not to kill you."

Bell nodded, her chin trembling as glassy tears welled in her eyes. Her voice cracked as she spoke in a barely audible whisper.

"I can tell you why you shouldn't kill me… but I don't think it's a good reason."

Her shoulders sagged, and the tears began to fall. She looked hollowed out, as if the story she was about to tell had already drained her soul.

"I made a deal with Zar," she said, her words filled with regret. "A deal for things I shouldn't have wanted."

The air in the room grew heavier. I watched the woman closely, sword still in hand, unsure if I was listening to a confession or a trap.

"I saw her," Bell continued, "a young woman at the library. She worked there. I'd see her sometimes, just in passing, but something about her… it pulled at me. My

41

heart ached in ways I didn't understand. I was unraveling. My husband was in the hospital, and I was drowning in grief. I didn't know who I was anymore."

She wiped her eyes with the back of her hand, smearing mascara across her cheek.

"I met Zar in the restroom. I was crying so hard I couldn't breathe. She came to me. Her voice was soft, and she had warm eyes. She didn't look like a demon. She looked human. Beautiful. Kind. She listened. Really listened. Even when I told her about... my feelings for a woman."

Staring at her, half-believing, half-bracing for something to burst from her. Was this a performance? A demon's manipulation? Or something else?

"She held my face," Bell said, as if she were watching the memory from far away. "She kissed me. It felt gentle... until I felt her teeth. She bit my lip. When she pulled away, there was blood on her tongue. She smiled and said, 'I know you will, Bell.' That was the deal. All I had to do was give someone a key."

Our eyes met, and hers were pleading. "I didn't ask questions. I just agreed. I was desperate. She promised I'd have what I wanted. As she left, she said, 'Oh, and if someone comes for the key... they might kill you. Or worse. Oops.'"

The laugh that came from Bell was hollow and broken.

"She said if no one came in five years, I'd be free, but if they did... I'd have to give them the key, and my life."

"You sold your soul to Zar... for love?"

She nodded, tears streaking her face. "You don't understand. Before Jasmine, I never looked at another woman. I was married. I was loyal, but everything changed when my husband was in the hospital. I was lost, and then I saw her smile."

Bell's voice softened. "She was younger than me, but her smile lit up the room. She helped me get a library card. She was kind. Gentle. When I bumped into her and dropped her books, she laughed. I helped her pick them up, and I caught her scent. It wasn't perfume. It was just... her. I breathed it in, and my heart felt alive again."

The intimacy of her words made me uncomfortable. "Can you hurry this up?"

She nodded, wiping her eyes. "Sorry. It's been months since I let myself think about her."

Bell continued, her voice growing quieter. "My husband was in a coma. Brain dead. His parents stopped me from pulling the plug; we fought about it, and they eventually won. We'd fallen out of love long before the accident. I had been praying for something to change, and then the accident happened. It was all my fault. I was alone, and then Zar came."

She paused to blow her nose.

"I told Zar everything. About my husband. His family. The library. Jasmine. She listened, and I gave her everything she asked for."

My patience was wearing thin. I needed to find Zar. "Woman, could you please hurry up and get to the point with this story already?"

She dipped her head and said, "Sorry, at first, I hoped you would never come, but after living in so much pain at what I had done, I long for my death."

"Where is Jasmine now? Does she live with you here?"

Bell looked at her trembling hands. "She died. Two years ago. Cancer. Fast. Brutal." She looked up, eyes hollow. "So, if you kill me... it doesn't matter. I deserve it. I have nothing left here."

Without warning, she reached for her blouse. The fabric tore, scattering buttons across the floor. She opened it, revealing a white lacey bra stretched across her chest. Between her breasts, a brass skeleton key hung from a chain, glinting in the light.

Unclasping the chain, she held it to me with a shaking hand.

"I kept my promise," she whispered. "I have the key, and if you want it… You can take my life, too."

She did not bother to cover herself as she stood there with tears falling, the bone-shaped metal dangling from her hand.

My heart sank even deeper, past pity and judgment. Whatever beauty she once carried had withered by despair as she trembled. She was a woman pleading for mercy. She was unraveling.

The brass key dangled from the chain, its cold gleam catching the light. "Why wear it around your neck?" I asked. "To keep the evil close to your heart? Or so she can keep an eye on you?"

Bell wiped her eyes again, further smearing mascara across her cheek. "No," she whispered. "The keychain broke at work yesterday. I didn't have time to fix it, and with everything happening in the streets… I couldn't risk it being stolen."

I nodded, still watching the key. "I thought maybe it meant something symbolic."

My fingers brushed the cool metal as I reached for it. It was heavier than I expected, worn and pitted with age. Scratches crisscrossed its surface, and beneath the grime, I saw faint letters etched into the brass.

REGRET

"What am I supposed to do with this?" I asked.

Bell's voice was barely audible. "Use it to find Zar. She's been waiting for you."

The cold metal turned over in my hand, as its edges bite into my palm. "Where's the door?"

"I don't know," she said. "She never told me. Just said

to give it to you."

A knot was forming in my chest. The key pulsed with a cold ancient presence. Bell saw the shift in my expression and recoiled.

"Now that you have it..." she whispered, "are you going to kill me?"

I blinked, startled. "What? No. I don't kill innocents."

She sobbed, her body folding in on itself. "But I'm not innocent. I wanted my husband dead. I wanted to be with someone else. I made a deal with a demon. I deserve this."

She collapsed into a fetal position, her body wracked with convulsions. Her cries grew louder, more desperate, until they became prayers. Broken and trembling words of the *Our Father* prayer spilled from her lips.

The air in the apartment shifted. A voice, deep, cold, and final, rippled through the room. "Too late."

I spun, sword raised, breath caught in my throat, but it was not Zar. Instead, it was another door.

Three feet away and hovering a foot above the ground, it had appeared without sound. It was a slab of pale white freezer-burned flesh, rimmed in frost. Mist curled from its edges, coiling around my boots and Bell's limp form. The temperature dropped, and my breath fogged in the air.

I stepped between Bell and the door, blade ready. I tapped the surface with the tip of my sword. The thing was solid, and where the steel touched, a bead of blood welled up and dripped from the icy face.

Frost scraped away with the blade. The cold shot through the sword and bit into my fingertips, until the word emerged: *regret*, etched deep into the door's skin.

No knob. No keyhole.

I knocked on the icy surface with the key, unsure of what else to do.

The sound echoed strangely, as if it had been swallowed. I waited, tense, unsure of what the answer would be.

A gentle voice, almost warm, drifted from within.

"Come on in."

The door lowered to the floor with a soft thud before creaking open slowly and deliberately. Bell stirred behind me, her sobs silenced. She shuffled backward and then fell. She had tripped on the carpet and hit her head, and her body crumpled against the wall. Her chest rose and fell, so she was alive, but out of the way. That pretty head would feel terrible in the morning.

"It's for the best."

The door was open now. Inside was a room bathed in soft white light. Bright enough to illuminate, but not enough to cast shadows. The air shimmered as I braced for an attack, muscles taut, sword raised.

A cool, dry breeze brushed past me, ruffling my clothes. It did not just touch me; it passed through me. My skin prickled, and my hair stood on end.

At first, a faint smell drifted past, reminiscent of dust and moth-riddled linen from my grandmother's attic. The scent shifted into the tang of copper. It filled my mouth with the taste of a penny, making me gag.

"Come on, Zar!" I shouted into the light. "I'm ready to end you!"

The scent changed again to that of rotten meat. My stomach was clenched. I staggered, and bile rose into my throat.

The door began to close.

"In or out?" the voice asked.

My jaw clenched as I forced my legs to sprint. The door slammed behind me with a sound.

I stood in a cold room that had been stripped of life. A feminine figure was perched on a splintered wooden barstool at the center. Her body was skeletal and draped in rags that clung to it like a second skin. The skin was burnt crimson, cracked, and peeling, and looked so brittle that a single breath might shred it into ribbons.

The woman's hair was a tangled nest of black filth, crawling with fat lice; the strands shifted as if they were stirring beneath her scalp. The stench of rot clung to her. Her arms were mottled with liver spots, some swollen and crusted with pus that oozed in sickly shades of green and yellow.

One bloodshot eye stared at me, rimmed in crust. The other was sewn shut with coarse black thread. Her hands dripped crimson, each droplet pooled around her on the floor, but then the blood rose, dripping upward as red rain in reverse, vanishing as it passed her head into a mist.

I raised my sword, the weight of it leveling me against the sight of madness. "Zar! Give me the mother and the child, and I'll walk away. Otherwise, I'll end you."

She lifted a bony hand, slicked with blood, and smiled a jagged grin of blackened, broken teeth. "That's my name," she rasped. "But you can call me Mistress Zar, boy."

I stepped closer, blade gleaming. "Release the mother and child. Free Bell from her contract. Or die."

A chill slithered through me, curling from my toes to my fingertips. My breath fogged. My skin prickled. Something deep inside whispered, *"This might be your last fight."* I pushed the thought away. "But I will not die first."

Zar's grin widened. "You might want to think about that... before you enter into my Madness." A bony finger pointed behind me.

Glancing around, the door still hung in the air, suspended. The plaque that once read *"Regret"* now bled, thick crimson rivulets spilling over the letters. As the blood drained, a new word emerged.

SSENDAM

Zar's voice turned mocking. "Oops. Too late. You're mine now to do as I wish. That sword may have slain my kin, but I am Mistress Zar. Do you remember the first demon you killed?"

Wooden boards slammed against the door, one after another, as if hurled by invisible hands. Nails drove themselves in with deafening cracks, sealing the exit. I spun toward Zar.

She was gone.

Only the stool remained, and the last of the blood was vanishing into the air. The temperature plummeted, causing goose bumps on my arms. My breath came in clouds, and my heartbeat thundered in my ears.

"You thought I'd let you leave that easily?" her voice echoed. "Regret not running when you had the chance?"

The lights flickered once, twice, before dying. Darkness swallowed everything. When they returned, the stool was occupied again, but not by Zar.

A porcelain clown doll sat there, no taller than a toddler. Its face was painted in a grotesque mimicry of innocence with rosy cheeks, smeared lipstick, and a grin full of needle-sharp teeth. Its eyes were black voids, glossy and lifeless, yet somehow watching.

My grip on the sword tightened as I swung it in wide arcs all around me, slicing through the air in hopes that I would catch Zar sneaking up on me. The room felt smaller, as if the walls were closer. The doll did not move, but I could feel it waiting.

I stepped closer, blade extended. The doll's face began to twist and warp like a baby's face stretched over a skull. I could feel those dark voids where its eyes should be watching, waiting.

Just as my sword neared its porcelain skin, the lights went out again.

Thump. Something hit the ground in front of me.

A high-pitched giggle broke the silence. The laughter was childlike, but something was off in the way it echoed around the room. It circled me, footsteps light and quick, the giggle rising into a twisted melody.

"Ring around the rosies…"

I turned, blade swinging, fighting the urge to panic.

"Pocket full of posies…"

Zar's voice boomed in my ears from the darkness.

"Do you think you can stop me? You think a human can kill me with a little knife? Do you, you little slug?"

The air vibrated with the demon's fury. The walls rattled around me. My skin crawled.

"I am a thing. A beast. Forged in hellfire after the Great War. I was born of sin, destruction, and hunger from the fires of hell. I live for the taste of human souls." The room grew colder. "Now is the time for me to fulfill what I was made for."

I swung my sword toward the sound, slicing through the thick, suffocating dark. The blade emitted a faint silver-white moonlight glow, but the darkness devoured it. Only a six-inch halo of light was left around me. Beyond that, nothing. No walls. No floor. Just void.

The air was so cold it was biting at my fingertips with icy teeth. My breath fogged. Yet my body burned as sweat trickled down my spine. I twisted and slashed, praying that it would hit anything at all.

High-pitched, giddy laughter came. The childlike

demon darted around me, giggling, slapping at my legs with tiny, stinging blows. I kicked and swung wildly, but hit nothing. The laughter danced through the air, mocking me.

A voice slithered through the dark silence that followed.

"How do you like my little pet?" she purred. "She's a special demon. Loves making children scream. Cry. Beg. I, on the other hand... I enjoy everyone. Big, small, black, brown, white, young, old. I'm a giver. I give until it hurts, and I savor every scream of pain like a delicious pleasure. Mmm..."

A spotlight snapped on. The sudden brightness was blinding. I recoiled, shielding my eyes. As they adjusted, I saw it was a single ghost light, the kind left burning on a theater stage after hours. It cast a pale circle of illumination across the front of the stage.

Zar stood beneath the light wearing a magician's costume with a top hat, cape, gloves, and all the trappings of illusion. The grin was too wide on her skeletal face.

At her feet lay a limp woman whose belly was swollen. She was sprawled across a black pillar of slick, oily stone that seemed to pulsate beneath her. A red haze surrounded her.

The woman did not move. Something was familiar about her, but I could not place it. It was a memory of a dream in another life. The way you might meet a stranger for the first time, but you are positive you have met them before.

The girl's eyes were settled on the haze, or through it. She trembled, blood trickling from scratches on her arms and legs. Tiny scratches. The size of a child's hand.

The porcelain demon had vanished the moment the light came on.

A soft, warm voice in my head spoke to me, and I felt

as if my soul was wrapped in a blanket fresh from the dryer. My eyes closed for a moment as I embraced this more comfortable sensation.

"When you are ready, call upon Guardian." The presence vanished before I could respond.

I opened my eyes. Zar was watching me, her expression twisted with mock confusion.

"Boy," she sneered, "there's no praying in here. It won't help you. In here, I am everything. Hope dies here."

Oversized teeth, yellowed and blackened at the roots, revealed themselves as she smiled wide. A sliver of fear crept into my spine, whispering doubt as her words lingered in my head.

She raised her hand as I was shoved hard from behind by a giant palm pressing between my shoulder blades. I stumbled forward, and the pinches came soon after. The hands were tiny, and the nails were sharp.

They climbed the backs of my legs, each one like needles. I grunted, biting back a scream. The pinches doubled with each attack, slicing through skin. Blood soaked into my shirt.

The tiny hands grabbed at my lower back as it began to climb.

I knew it was the porcelain demon. The diminutive monster pulled itself up, its tiny fingers digging into my skin. It reached my shoulders, yanking my hair so hard I felt strands rip free. The pain in my scalp eclipsed everything else. My knees buckled. My left side went numb.

The demon bounced on my shoulder with the weight of a cinder block. I staggered, teeth clenched, vision swimming as my head turned to see the thing.

Its face was twisted with glee, and its eyes wide like a child about to unwrap a gift.

Zar was placing her hand on the pregnant woman's belly as I returned my attention to her.

The woman's clothes began to glow deep crimson, the color of fresh blood. They ignited. Flames licked across the fabric, consuming it in seconds, but her skin remained untouched, with no burns, no blisters, only a layer of ash.

A raw, primal scream tore through the room from her throat. I met her gaze, and her eyes met mine. They were filled with agony. With sorrow. With fading hope.

My faith battled against the rising doubts inside me. I felt her pain in my bones. In my soul.

She turned her head, looking at Zar, searching for mercy. Zar only grinned back at her; there was no mercy in the demon's eyes.

I stepped forward, blood dripping from my back. My scalp burned, and my shoulder was numb.

"Don't give up hope," I said. It was a struggle to speak, but nothing would stop me. I had not lost hope yet. "I'll find a way to save you, and the baby."

Zar leaned over the woman, the grin stretching her cracked lips into a mask of cruelty. Her eyes were black pits rimmed in red and locked onto the pregnant woman's face. The demon was drinking in her terror. The woman trembled beneath her, her throat convulsing with silent screams, tears spilling across her cheeks and pooling in the grime below.

The cavernous mouth gaped open, as a serpent preparing to swallow its prey whole. She hovered with her breath reeking of sulfur and rotten meat. A thick stream of green sludge dripped from her long, pointed tongue. The waxy slime splattered on the woman's face, trailing down her cheeks.

The ooze continued to flow, coating her body in slow, viscous streaks. The sludge clung to her skin like tree sap, glistening under the dim light, trapping her in a cocoon of filth. She squirmed as her lips formed a desperate plea, but no sound escaped except the hollow gasp of someone drowning in fear.

Zar's long tongue slithered out as it tasted the air. She slumped closer, letting the long muscle tendril trace the contours of the woman's face, smearing the green muck into a glistening slime. The scent was the same nauseating blend that had clung to the door when I first arrived.

The woman convulsed as Zar's hand hovered above her, with fingertips painting her with the slime. She caressed the breast, her nails dragging through the slime, leaving behind grooves that steamed in the cold air. Her touch was slow and deliberate.

Zar's hand slid from her neck to her groin, tracing goosebumps. She rested her fingers just above the birth canal. She looked at me with a grin that split her face. "What lovely breasts," she cooed. "So ripe. So full of white, liquid sweetness."

A bony finger circled one breast and scraped away a layer of slime, revealing flushed skin. The woman moaned with a low, guttural sound, more animal than human. Her eyes fluttered, on the edge of unconsciousness.

Zar frowned and pinched the nipple hard. The woman twisted in agony, and a thin stream of milk sprayed from the nipple, splashing onto Zar's face. The demon's tongue darted around, lapping it up with greedy delight. She closed her eyes, savoring the taste, then opened them again wider and darker.

The demon turned to me. "Want some?" she whispered. "You know you do."

I snarled. "Bring me closer. It'll make it easier to kill you."

Zar chuckled and turned to the woman, her hand

creeping toward her belly. The woman's eyes snapped open. Realization came to her that her baby was in danger as Zar's other hand had slid to rest on her stomach.

The tongue flicked across her face, savoring each whimper. The woman's body was shaking. Her lips moved in silent prayer, begging for death, for release.

The demon's eyes stayed locked on mine, feeding off the rage building in my chest. She licked the milk from her breast and pried open her mouth with ease. The woman resisted, but her jaw slackened, as if her soul had already begun to slip away.

Zar's tongue plunged inside, writhing like a starving animal. The woman's eyes rolled in their sockets as her body went limp.

Five feet away, sword trembling in my grip. "I'm closer now, you piece of…"

The demon on my shoulder bounced, giggling and clapping. Each bounce sent a jolt of pain through my spine, nearly dropping me to my knees.

The woman gagged awake, and her voice was raw and broken. "No, Lord… please… save my baby… please end this madness…"

Zar hissed. "In here, madness is law. Life is meaningless. I am mistress of this place. Sin is my feast. Blood is my soup. Flesh is my candy."

She leaned closer to the woman. "I see your fear. I tasted it. It makes me shiver with delight in intimate places. I'm wet with your desperation."

I growled. "You had your chance. Now you die."

Zar laughed. "You think I'm holding you back? No. It's your fear that has kept you from attacking. You want to feel my power. You crave its embrace."

The demon on my shoulder nodded. Each bounce of the tiny bastard felt like a hammer blow. I staggered and bent double.

My eyes closed and I prayed. A soft, warm, childlike voice whispered in my mind. "Don't lose hope."

Daisy's voice warmed my chest, spreading through my limbs. The pain in my back and shoulders dulled. The fear receded, and I understood now. Zar was not holding me. It was me, just as she had claimed.

Getting closer to embracing her power was not my plan. I wanted to touch the pregnant girl to give the woman what Zar could never understand. The hope that I carried into hell with me.

Although my limbs remained paralyzed, the sword was still warm in my grip. It felt alive, as if it sensed the nearness of its mark. Power thrummed through the blade, aching to be unleashed, but Zar and the porcelain demon did not flinch. They either did not fear the weapon or believed I was too broken to wield it.

Zar's mocking voice drifted through the air. "In here, I am no simple demon. I am Zar. Mistress of Madness."

She spread her arms, her grin stretching unnaturally across her face. The air behind her convulsed, and a wind erupted that was hot and cold at once. The gust slammed into me, tearing at my clothes, stinging my skin. Her body began to twist, contorting like a rag wrung dry, but instead of water, blood gushed from her pores.

The crimson splashed across the stage, the woman, and me. Wherever it landed, it vanished, absorbed into the skin, into the wood, into the stone. It hit me like glass shards piercing every inch of my flesh.

The woman screamed, and her voice cracked. Her body spasmed beneath the torrent. She had no understanding of what was happening. I barely did.

My head whipped around searching for an escape, for any crack in the madness. Zar stopped what she was doing and shouted over the little demon squealing on my shoulder.

"There are no doors here," she said, her tone gleeful. "Only one window. A window for others to watch the madness I possess, but that window is not for you. Even if you could crawl through it, you would find what lingers there far more terrifying than me."

She began to sing a song under her breath as she stared down at the pregnant woman.

"Swim with rocks as the night stomps on the trees,
Leaves dance their way to the ground, broken memories tease,
Of what it's like to hate life, they laugh.
Sing a happy tune with smiles in your sleep,
I'll whisper the truths that make you weep,
And tell you all the things that make you hate the world."

Her words were nonsense. They did not even rhyme or follow a rhythm, but they wormed into my mind.

The doll on my shoulder leaned in, its breath sour and damp against my ear as its squeaky voice wormed its way down my ear canal. "The world hates you, and you hate yourself."

I collapsed in pain that curled through my gut. My insides twisted, and my muscles seized. Zar continued to twist herself into impossible knots, and I grew hot with anger, confusion, and despair. My mind swirled into madness.

The pain pinned me down. The little demon was no longer on my shoulder. It sat in front of me, legs crossed, and clapping. Its smile was wide, with cracked porcelain teeth, and black-painted eyes gleamed with delight.

My eyes shut, trying to focus my thoughts on breathing and keep whatever is left in my stomach from coming up.

The demon stood and circled me as I braced for impact. The tiny bastard came fast with sharp blows to my knees, my thighs, each one was a hammer wrapped in razors. It slashed several times until I swung the sword back towards it, and it vanished into the shadows. When I turned back to Zar, the doll was sitting and waiting again.

A voice returned to my head that sounded like my own voice, but this time it was darker, colder, and more malicious.

"I'm a monster. A burden. An embarrassment. My grandmother wished the dark figure had killed me so she could live her life without all my problems. My parents are ashamed. I should be buried in a place no one would ever find me, not that anyone would even search for me if I were missing."

My parents and my grandma chanted all around me, "We hate you. We wish you were dead. We wish you had never been born. Die! Die! Do the right thing. You know what you need to do. Kill yourself."

Tears welled, and my throat burned deep in my chest. The voices did not stop. They echoed, multiplied, until my thoughts were no longer mine. I vomited, the stench rising thick and sour, coating my throat and nostrils.

My mind was spinning as the voices cried out that I should suffer for my sins. A sense of dread fell over me as I wondered why I had ever been born. What was my purpose in life other than being alone? Why did it matter? I should not have been born at all. I have nothing to live for, and I'm surrounded by misery and death.

"I wish I had died at birth. I wish I were dead. I wish that someone would kill me before I take another breath. I hope that killing myself puts an end to everyone's problems. That is what I want."

The smell and burn of vomit dripping from my nose and lips choked me, and the fog in my head cleared.

The voices were not inside me. They were Zar's.

Projected. Manipulated.

I clung to the stench, to the physical revulsion, and used it to anchor myself. The memory of why I was here replayed in my head. Gradually, the voices faded.

The woman sobbed nearby, her cries hollow and defeated. Zar and the demon were gone. Everything was shrouded in darkness, yet her tears continued to fall.

My heart was pounding in my chest as I struggled to stand. Deep laughter echoed around me. An icy breeze curled around me, and a voice whispered, "How is your mother?"

The darkness pressed in. My eyelids squeezed shut, and I remembered the night they told me she was gone. That night, I dreamt I was four again. Alone in my room. Crying. Waiting for her to come, hold me. She was supposed to protect me, but she never came. I prayed that someone would come.

There were five soft knocks on the closet door.

I whispered, "Come in."

Light spilled from beneath the door. Two shadows moved inside, slow and deliberate.

My heart pounded, and my ears strained for any clue to who it was.

The doorknob turned with a slow, deliberate click. It stopped, and the door creaked open a little. The light vanished. My pupils dilated, searching for any trace of illumination. Then came a dry and guttural cackle rising from the closet from a throat that sounded as if it had not breathed in centuries.

It started as a wheeze, before the laugh twisted into a helium-laced giggle, shrill and malicious. My bladder gave way. The sound was worse than any scream a human could make.

The voice sounded too familiar. This was the doll demon. The one that had been tormenting me. The one that had somehow stitched its voice into my nightmares.

Even in the dark, I opened my eyes and screamed in defiance. "Zar! I am here to send you back to the pit you crawled from! Show yourself!"

The ghost light snapped on, casting a pale, theatrical glow across the stage. It focused on the woman's bare, swollen belly, her skin slick with sweat and streaked with blood. Behind her, perched on a squat wooden stool, stood the porcelain clown demon. The little figure was dressed in a ringmaster's garb, its arms raised as if it were about to announce the opening act.

My torso moved, but my arms remained locked in place. Rage surged through me, burning out the last traces of fear. The woman screamed once and collapsed into unconsciousness.

The clown held its pose, frozen like a macabre figurine. A smile spread, revealing tiny rows of jagged teeth. It climbed down from the stool, its limbs bending at unnatural angles, and crawled onto the woman's belly. The demon circled once, twice, as a dog preparing to sleep, and curled up with eyes closed.

A hot, slimy pressure landed on the back of my neck.

Spinning instinctively, my body moved before my mind caught up. I swung my sword, slicing in a wide arc, but hit nothing.

Zar was suddenly there, kneeling beside the woman, stroking the sleeping demon as if it were a cherished pet. Her fingers moved with eerie tenderness, her eyes locked onto mine.

"I'll need a plaything," she whispered. "Would you like to be mine, Adam? My concubine? I'll bleed you until you pass out, then nurse you back to health... to do it again."

She pouted, raising three fingers like a scout's oath, and traced a heart over her chest. "I promise I'll be faithful."

A snarl escaped my lips. "Zar! I told you, I will destroy you and that worthless little demon!"

The demon's smile grew wider as she leaned and licked the woman's breast, trailing her fingers through the patch of hair between her legs. "You wouldn't hurt your little sister, would you?"

My breath caught. No. That could not be true.

The woman looked too young, barely twenty years old. My mother had always said she wished she had a daughter. My parents had called me a miracle child, born despite the trauma she suffered as a girl when a hit-and-run driver had struck her. My mother could not have had another. Could she?

But the resemblance... The woman looked similar to me when I had a clean shave.

My head spun and I staggered, dizzy with doubt.

"She can't be my sister!" I shouted. "I don't have one! Stay out of my head!"

Zar chuckled, blood dripping from her lips, splattering across the woman's chest. "You don't know she isn't, but I just wanted to see your face."

The demon smeared the blood, painting her.

"This is your half-sister," she said, voice syrupy with malice. "And she's carrying your niece. Soon, she'll be mine, and the baby... well, my little friend will take care of that."

The clown demon melted. Its porcelain skin liquefies, seeping into the woman's belly. Her skin rippled as it absorbed the creature like a sponge.

"No!" I shouted. "She's not my sister! I have no siblings!"

Zar's voice turned venomous. "Did you think your mother was the only one your father touched? He was as filthy as she was. She died screwing someone for ten dollars. A cheap whore. Mmm... how does that taste?"

A violent anger burned within my ribs. I gripped my sword tighter, imagining it buried in the demon's throat.

"You can't hurt my pet now," she said. "And soon, you won't be able to hurt me either. I'm about to take over your sissy's body, and what a body it is…"

I screamed, "You're full of lies! I will save the baby, the woman, and Bell. I'll enjoy watching you die!"

Zar laughed as her form liquefied into a pool of green and yellow water around the woman. Within a breath, the rotten water vanished into the girl's flesh just as the clown had.

Silence fell across the stage, and the ghost light flickered. The woman's eyes snapped open. They were two bottomless voids, black as coal and glistening like oil. She turned her head toward me with a slow, deliberate grace, her lips parting in a smile. The demon's tongue slithered across her lips, leaving behind a slick sheen of crimson saliva, and she rose from the stone slab with a languid, serpentine motion, her body trembling with unnatural allure.

She moved with sultry motions, her limbs fluid and boneless, but beneath the surface, I saw it: the twitch of pain in her muscles, the tremor of a soul still trapped inside. Her smile widened, eyes locked onto mine, and she began to walk toward me, hips swaying, her blood-slicked skin glistening under the ghost light's pale glow. I knew Zar was in control, but the girl was still alive in there.

Her hands roamed her own body with theatrical indulgence. One hand pinched and rolled her nipples, the other caressed her swollen belly, smearing blood in lazy spirals. Iron and rot filled the air with a stench, mingling with the sour musk of sweat.

"Do you see something you want to taste?" she purred. "Or do you want it all?"

I met her gaze, unflinching. "No. I do not lust for women like some dog. You won't tempt me."

Pausing mid-step, her body swayed. The fingers moved with practiced rhythm, tracing curves and creases, her eyes searching mine for weakness, but I gave her nothing.

The demon was six feet away when her smile faltered. Her eyes narrowed, and the mask of seduction cracked. Something ancient and cruel stirred beneath her skin. The woman's face twitched, flashing jagged teeth and a shimmer of rotten flesh, revealing a glimpse of her true form.

She stopped an arm's length from me, her breath hot and sour, and her scowling eyes. "Boy," she hissed, "do you think you can kill me? I told you, I am Mistress of this domain. I do the killing here."

The woman's voice was soft and intimate, as if she were sharing a dirty secret. My arms loosened. The sword buzzed in my grip, eagerly, but I hesitated. She was right. This was her realm.

With a grin on my face, I willed the sword to return to its ring form. Her eyebrows lifted in mock surprise, her grin returning with renewed confidence.

"I told you I'd kill you," I said, "but you know I'm not strong enough to do it here, don't you?"

The demon-possessed woman stepped closer, her body brushing mine, her skin slick and feverish. One of her hands trailed down the front of my jeans, the other curled around my back, with fingers digging into my flesh. The swollen belly pressed against me. The baby within was warm and kicking, and I could feel that the life within it was unnatural.

She leaned in, her breath damp on my ear. "You're going to love the way this hurts," she whispered. "You'll beg for more. I promise not to be gentle."

"But you won't love the way I punish you."

The demon pulled back, eyes searching mine, her hands sliding to the small of my back. "What do you mean, lover? I have you."

I wrapped my arms around her, gripping tight. "No," I said, voice low and steady. "I have you, dummy."

The possessed woman stiffened. She tried to escape, but I held fast, gripping my wrists behind her. The sickly form twisted, her nails raked my skin, but she was too close to strike with enough force to break my hold. Her breath turned to snarls, and her eyes flared with fury.

Even demons, when bound to flesh, were subject to the flesh's limits.

She sank her teeth into my shoulder. Pain ripped through me. A scream launched from my throat and echoed through the chamber.

"Guardian!" I roared. "I call upon you!"

A blinding burst of light erupted around us in a kaleidoscope of colors. Violet, crimson, gold, and electric blue exploded as a thousand firework shows blended into one. A living force of heat and vibration rippled through the air and made the ground tremble beneath my feet.

Zar shrieked, her borrowed body twisting against mine. Her skin grew fever-hot, slick with blood and sweat, as she thrashed in a desperate attempt to shed the human shell she had possessed. The demon's limbs jerked, and I felt the heat of her rage radiating through me as if it were a hot coal pressed against my skin.

The wind howled through the chamber like a divine hurricane, deafening and absolute as it tore through the colors, stripping them away in a blur. Zar's mouth moved, her lips curled in fury, but her curses were swallowed whole by the roar. I only felt her clawing at me and slicing my skin with every ounce of strength she had.

Blood poured from my wounds, warm and wet,

soaking my clothes and pooling at my feet. My vision blurred, I became lightheaded, but I refused to let go. Not yet.

As abruptly as it began, the wind stopped.

Zar broke free, stumbling, her face twisted in rage. "What did you do?" she spat. "Did you think a gust of wind and a light show could defeat me? I'll devour your flesh and torment your soul for eternity! I am Zar, Mistress of my Domain!"

My knees collapsed as the pain and blood loss dragged me down. My fingers trembled. My breath came in ragged gasps. I could not think, could not move until a voice whispered in my mind.

"Now."

I summoned the sword with a quick tap on the ring. The weapon materialized in my hand, bursting with celestial energy, and I hurled it skyward. The blade soared ten feet into the air, hovered for a heartbeat, and began to descend.

Zar laughed a guttural, bone-rattling sound that echoed through the chamber. "You missed me!" she roared, her eyes gleaming with triumph.

"I didn't throw it at you," I said with a smirk. "I returned it to its rightful owner, and we're not in your domain anymore, stupid." I shouted past Zar, "Guardian! I return your sword to you!"

Zar's smile faltered as her eyes darted around the room. She inhaled, a deep, guttural breath meant to fuel another roar, but it caught in her throat. Blood splattered from her mouth, and her expression twisted into terror.

The demon staggered, clutching her throat, as she looked up.

The sword was held by a mighty arm extended from the light of the fireworks that still surrounded us. The arm was wrapped in radiant golden armor. The fingers curled around the hilt. Behind Zar stood Guardian with her wings unfurled, her eyes blazing with righteous fury. The blade hovered above Zar's head, glowing with a pulsating fiery blue light.

Zar's face began to unravel, her human disguise melting away. The skin cracked, revealing scales and sinew. Her eyes turned to pits of shadow. The demon lunged, slashing at the armored arm, but her blows were as deadly as feathers slapping against stone. She leapt again, desperate, but Guardian did not flinch.

The demon landed, panting, her body grotesque and monstrous and still pregnant. She circled the archangel, her claws twitching, a tail extending behind her, and whipped with a crack.

Guardian stood tall, her voice calm. "It's been a long time, sister."

Zar snarled, her voice rough and broken. "Yes, it has been... Seven hundred years since I last knocked you down, ape-lover. You think you can defeat me? This sword is nothing. I'll heal and destroy you both."

The archangel smiled. "I've learned a few things since then, and I have friends." She withdrew the outstretched sword and stood tall.

From the shadows behind the demon, soft giggles echoed. They were childlike and innocent. Zar's form flickered, reverting to the face of the young woman. She wrapped her arms around herself, tears welling in her eyes.

The woman looked at me. "Brother... help me. They want to hurt me and your niece. We're family. Please..."

My face was stone, unmoved. "She's not my niece, and you're not my sister, bitch."

Three boys and two girls stepped from the darkness, their eyes filled with light. They placed their hands on Zar's body. The possessed woman screamed, and I was sure she would toss the tiny cherubs around like rag dolls.

The woman thrashed about, attempting to escape. The demon clawed and kicked, but the kids remained still. It was as if she could not strike or shove them away. Their touch was gentle, but it held her like iron. Smoke rose from her skin. The stench of rot filled the air, along with the smell of burnt hair, sour flesh, and decay.

She shrieked, "If you kill me, the baby dies! Bell dies!"

The demon laughed, triumphant, believing she had won.

I looked at Guardian, who met my gaze, her smile reassuring. The angel knew what I was thinking. She had seen the sword's power and knew what it cost. Every demon I had ever slain with the sword had been destroyed, even the humans that they had possessed rarely survived the blade. I only took comfort in taking those lives because their souls had been saved and sent to Heaven.

The angel turned to Zar. "I told you, I've learned. This sword only destroys when wielded by a human, but in my hands…"

Guardian raised the blade with both hands. The weapon flared, burning with blue flames, casting shadows that danced like spirits around the void. I had never seen it shine that brightly for me.

"I only want it to destroy you and the abomination you carry."

The blade sliced through the air, striking Zar's chest with a flash so bright it seared my vision. The woman's body exploded with no sound, only light, followed by a scream.

Zar's death cry echoed around me, vibrating my bones, crawling across my skin. The children joyfully retreated, clapping and cheering.

Guardian stepped away from the woman's body. The

possession broke. The woman was dazed, but her eyes were clearing. She knelt with her quivering hands cradling her belly. They were free, and the nightmare was over.

Her skin was pale and glistening with sweat and residual slime as she sat motionless. There were no visible wounds, but her eyes were unblinking, glassy, and unfocused. Her fingers trembled as they reached for her head, then her belly, as if trying to confirm that she was still whole. Breath came in shallow gasps, each one fogging the cool air around her.

She blinked, and the awareness crept back in. Her gaze dropped to her bare body, and a flush of red spread across her cheeks. The woman tried to cover herself, but her hands were slick with drying slime and blood, and she could barely manage the gesture.

I turned to Guardian, whose radiant form still shimmered with light. "What happened? Why isn't she dead?" I asked, my voice hoarse, and the taste of iron still thick in my mouth.

Guardian's smile was calm, almost maternal. "The sword was mine first," she said. "And I've learned a few things since Zar and I last met. I can now destroy those who rebelled against our Father without destroying the innocent form they possess."

The weight of her words settles into my chest. "And the baby? Or Bell? Will they be okay?"

Guardian's eyes glowed. "The mother and child are safe. Bell is healing. Our Father sees great things ahead."

I exhaled, and the tension in my shoulders eased. "But Bell signed her soul away. How can she be free?"

Guardian raised her hand, revealing a rolled parchment curled in her giant palm. "You mean this?"

The contract dissolved into dust, scattering on a breeze. I watched the final tether to Zar's dominion undone.

"I have so many questions," I said. "How did the children hold Zar? How did you destroy her? How did you pull us out of Madness? And... is this woman really my sister?"

Before Guardian could answer, a voice behind me said, "The only answers we're allowed to give are the ones our Father permits, and right now he says we must have faith. He loves us."

Jacob and Knox stood in the soft glow of the aftermath, their faces calm and composed.

Knox stepped forward. "It only took a blink of an eye for Guardian to bring you here, and yes, she is your sister. Her mother told her your name, but not how to find you. She has no one else."

I looked at them all and felt the gravity of choice settle on my shoulders. "It felt like forever to get here," I said. "But yes, I'll help her. I'll help anyone who needs it." I took a deep breath as the responsibility started to weigh on me. "I'd be proud to protect my family. What's her name?"

Guardian's smile deepened. "Her name is Helen, and the baby... she'd like to be called Tara."

"How do you know?" I asked.

"I just do."

I nodded. "Helen and Tara. I'll do my best to take care of them."

Guardian extended a robe, white and glowing, the fabric whispering as it shifted in her hand. I took it and knelt beside Helen. The poor woman flinched at the touch, her eyes still clouded with confusion.

"Who are you?" she whispered. "Why are you helping me?"

I wrapped the robe around her, the fabric warm against her chilled skin. "I'm your brother. Adam."

Helen's eyes searched mine, dazed and uncertain. "Are

you the one my mother told me about?"

"Yes," I said, helping her to her feet. "And I'll be here for you and Tara."

"Tara?" she asked.

"My niece."

She leaned into me, her body soft and trembling, her head resting on my shoulder. I guided her to Guardian, who raised the sword once more.

"It's yours again, if you want it," she said. "If you take it, we'll meet again."

The hilt is warm in my hand, the blade humming with power. "I'll help those who need it."

Guardian nodded. "In your darkest moment, pray. If He allows it, I'll come."

"Thank you, I will always pray to our Father for forgiveness." I paused. "I thought you weren't allowed to help me defeat Zar, but you cut her down."

"Only Knox and Jacob were forbidden. I am neither."

I laughed. "Sneaky, Guardian. I get it, now. You also couldn't just go into Zar's hell because you needed me to pull her out."

She grinned, and I turned to the children. They had gathered around Knox and Jacob, their small hands clutching robes and sleeves. I waved to them.

"Thank you," I said. "May your waiting end soon. Knox, hopefully, I don't see you too soon, and Jacob, I hope Tara gives you a name that suits your sneakiness".

Knox and Jacob smiled.

Jacob added, "When Tara turns sixteen, there'll be a little car issue. Go easy."

"What? What kind of car issue are you talking about?"

Before the answer came, Guardian raised her arms. The wind rushed around us. In a blink, I was home.

Helen lay in my arms, breathing softly. I placed her in my bed and covered her with my Marilyn Monroe blanket. Tears welled in my eyes as I realized that Grandma and I were her only family now.

She began to snore, a quiet, rhythmic sound that filled the room with a sense of peace.

I walked to my desk, unlocked the drawer, and retrieved my writing materials. I ripped out a blank page and began to write. I needed to send a letter before I wrote in my journal again. It's been a while since I have written anything other than a college essay.

"Dear Grandma,

I'm sending you a friend who needs a place to stay. I'll need to do a little convincing, but he's going to help you out on the farm. He has an adorable little friend named Pancake that will help keep the foxes out of the chicken coop.

You'll love them, but guess what else I found out..."

LITTLE NIA

All stories have beginnings, but this one began a long time ago, and it does not start with a birth or a prophecy. This little slice of the story begins at 2:50 a.m. A time when the world forgets itself, when even the shadows seem to sleep.

Tick... tock.

Tick... tock.

The hour approaches. At 3:00 a.m., it begins.

A whisper drifted in the air that is not heard so much as felt. It leaked from the cracks on the pavement, from the seams in the walls, from the places where the streetlight dared not reach. The murmur was everywhere and nowhere.

A thick fog crept in, curling around curbs and gutters, swallowing sidewalks and fences. The misty air moved with silent purpose, carrying a chill that bit to the bone.

From the fog, as it drifted in and out of the alleys between apartment buildings, a song began.

It was a child's voice, but sung through a mouth full of mud. The melody is playful, but the voice is venomous.

Sing with me, little children, sing with me and tell me how much you love to play...
Sing with me, children, and watch me eat your soul today...

The fog expanded, climbing the sides of the buildings and licking at the cracked windows. The song grew louder, more gleeful, as if the singer were dancing in circles, drunk on its own cruelty.

Sing with me, little children, so you don't run away...
Sing with me, children, as I eat your flesh away...

Thin sheets of ice formed on rusted mailboxes, on the brittle leaves of dying trees. The air turned thick and suffocating as the fog became denser with every verse.

Now cry, little children, as I play with your fear...
Sing with me, children, as I feast upon your soul, ever near...

The voice giggled, high and cracked, as the song grew more jovial. It repeated the verses with increasing amusement as the fog engulfed the buildings, blocking all the light from the moon and streetlamps, casting a bitter cold darkness.

The presence found its destination. It was a rundown seven-story apartment building with bricks stained from decades of neglect. The fire escapes were rusty, and the lobby door lacked a lock. This was not a place that criminals paid attention to, because it was the home of sorrow, hanging in the suffocating air of life that existed within.

The fog wrapped it like a lover, pressing against the walls, seeping into the mortar. Trash in the street blew at the edges of the building opposite, caught by the breeze. It climbed, floor by floor, until it reached the top. A presence in the fog drifted around the windows of all fourteen apartments, slipping inside.

At a small window on the seventh floor, the fog curled and recoiled, as if testing the glass. Inside, the apartment was still. In the master bedroom, the parents slept peacefully in each other's arms, unaware of the thing pressing against their world.

In the smaller room, the fog lingered but did not enter. The room was a garden of innocence. Yellow and pink flowers bloomed across curtains, bedspreads, and wallpaper. A soft nightlight glowed at the head of the bed, casting a warm halo that pushed back the dark just enough.

Nia slept there. Four years old, her breath soft and steady, her arms wrapped around Lula, her stuffed lioness. Her smile was faint, the kind that only dreams can conjure.

A light clicked, not loud, but could have been as loud as a trumpet in the quiet room. The latch on the closet door shifted, and the doorknob began to turn slow.

Nia's leg twitched with a jolt of fear sparking through her nerves. The door creaked open a fraction, and the fog outside swirled, as if in anticipation. Night after night, it had come to watch the plague of terror.

Her fingers dug into the fabric of the comforter as her arms tightened around it. The eyelids of the little girl fluttered open, just barely. Holding her breath as she scanned the room. The presence knew she would pretend to be asleep.

The closet door was ajar. The girl stared at it, unmoving, her body rigid beneath the covers. Her heart drummed in her ears. The child wanted to see her mother or hear her father's voice, but as the door opened wider, none of her hopes came true.

Silence escaped her lips as the door creaked open a

little more.

Her lips moved, but her words were trapped. "M-M-M-Mom... D-D-D-Dad..." she whispered, her throat clenched with terror.

Warmth spread beneath her as her bladder lost control, but she did not notice. She wanted to run, to scream, to wake up, but fear held her captive.

Even her dolly, Lula, could not save her.

The voice came from the dark closet, from the place where nightmares were born.

"Knock, knock... Guess who's here, Princess."

It was deep and gurgling as if spoken through a throat full of broken glass and bile.

Nia shook, her teeth clattering. Tiny fists clenched the comforter, with her knuckles pale against the pink fabric.

She tried to scream. "M-M-M-M-Mom... D-D-D-Da..."

Her voice was a breathless whisper, barely louder than the rustle of her trembling sheets. Her voice could not pierce the two closed doors, the hum of the ceiling fan, or the soft snoring of her parents just twenty feet away. To Nia, they felt a world away.

Tears squeezed from her eyes, soaking into the pillow. Her bladder emptied again, the warmth spreading beneath her, and mixing with the cold sweat that clung to her skin.

Nia tried again to call out, but her voice was trapped. Lips moved, mouthing desperate pleas. "Mommy, help me... Daddy, please...", but no sound came. Her heart pounded.

She wanted safe arms around her, but only the silence answered her cries.

Her thoughts spiraled. Maybe she was bad. Perhaps they did not love her. Possibly, this was punishment for spilling milk or forgetting to put her dolly away. Her chest ached with guilt she could not name, her four-year-old mind searching for reasons that did not exist.

The closet door creaked open another inch. Time slowed. Each tear felt like a minute. Each twitch of Nia's limbs is like an hour. Her body is soaked, her muscles locked in terror, her breath shallow and fast. She is in a tiny storm of panic, trapped in a bed that once felt safe.

Her mouth moved as she cried. "Mommy, help me, please, mommy! Mom, please help, I need you!! Daddy, save me! Where are you, Daddy? Daddy! Please, I need your help! Mommy, where are you…"

She did not realize her screams were only in her mind, and the room was silent.

An electric pain shot through her chest as her little heart pounded against her ribs, as if to escape its prison. Horror filled her with the thought of her parents' betrayal. Why had they not come?

Soft, sorrowful words bubbled up from her tiny lips. "Mommy, I am sorry for being so bad. Forgive me."

Her body went limp, and she felt as if she had run a hundred miles.

Three soft taps on the inside of the half-open closet door echoed in the tiny room, like a child knocking to be let in.

A voice followed; the same voice that traveled with the fog.

Hush little baby, don't say a word…
Momma's going to buy you a mockingbird…
Oh, little baby, poor little baby, please be afraid…

The melody drifted across the room. The voice tried to be gentle, like a lullaby, but every syllable was soaked in malice.

"I hope you didn't forget about me. Did your parents

tell you I wasn't real? Was I just a bad dream? They lied. They hate you. You've ruined their lives, stolen their dreams. They called me to take care of bad little girls like you."

Something giggled in the darkness.

"I'm here to take you to a place where pain never ends. A hell where you will suffer for a very long time. I promised I'd come back, didn't I, little bitch? Ta-da..."

From the shadows of the closet, a hand emerged.

It was long and meaty, the skin split and peeling, revealing sinew and blackened muscle beneath. Three fingers extended, each wrapped in strips of necrotic flesh that oozed a thick, tar-like sludge. The yellow curvy nails grew as the fingers stretched.

The hand rested on the carpet, sinking into the plush fibers. Curling claws gripped the floor, pulling itself forward. It sounded as if soaked towels were being dragged across the floor, accompanied by low, wheezing grunts, as if the creature were breathing through a crushed windpipe.

The arm followed, muscles stringy and taut, stretching like rubber bands on the verge of snapping. More sludge poured from its joints, but it did not seem bothered by the loss of its fluids.

The head rose. A skull, half-deflated and gourd-shaped, pushed through the veil of shadow. Its skin matched the hand, slick, blistered, and torn. Three eyes bulged from its face, two set wide apart, pulsing with blue veins as thick as tentacles that writhed. The third eye sat crookedly above the others, twitching with excitement.

Its mouth was a cavern of broken teeth, jagged and brown, framing a fat, blistered tongue that lolled out. The creature grinned with a grotesque, gleeful expression of hunger.

The monster dragged itself further into the room, its

torso tapering into a mess of dangling innards that had been chewed, mangled, battered, smashed, and trailing behind like a butcher's scraps. It was as if the demon had been torn in half. No legs. No feet. Just a half-formed horror inching toward the pink bed.

Nia's heartbeat softly now, each thump a whisper. Her body was limp, her mind fading, but even in terror, she wondered why they did not come. Why did they not love her?

Was she not their little girl? Their joy. Their miracle?

Tears fell silently, soaking into the sheets. Did she spill the milk too often, or was it because she always forgot to put her dolly away before bedtime? She wanted forgiveness. She tried to be good. She wanted one more chance.

The half-creature reached the edge of the bed. The demon turned its misshapen head toward the corner of the room, its grin widening.

"Hello, Thomas," it rasped. "It's been a long time. Fifteen years, if I remember right."

From the corner, a shimmering light emerged as soft as moonlight. The light parted the curtain of shadows, revealing a figure no taller than a child. He looked to be seven, maybe younger, with round, cherubic features, but his body was not solid. He hovered a few inches from the floor. His wings, translucent and feathered with light, fluttered behind him. A glowing white gown draped around him, similar to the ones babies were baptized in.

His cheeks were flushed, streaked with tears that shimmered. His eyes are solemn. He appeared as someone watching a loved one slip away, again.

"Yes, Kay-aR," he whispered, his voice trembling. "It has been a long time. When you took my last ward, and now… now you're about to take this one. Just like before, I am forbidden to stop you."

The creature giggled. "Yes," it hissed, dragging its bloated form closer to the bed, its claws gouging the carpet with each pull.

Thomas lowered his head, his misty form flickering. He raised his hands in a desperate prayer. "Please, Father... free me from this bond. Let me protect her. I must protect her."

Kay-aR snorted. Its breath reeked of rot and sulfur. "Hush, Thomas," it crooned. "You're spoiling my joy. The anticipation of her pain is delicious. Don't worry, little girl, I'll be there soon. I'm so happy to have the honor of taking her soul. So many possibilities for torture."

Thomas stepped into the shadows, his glow dimmed, with his head bowed in silent defeat. Kay-aR's claws curled around the leg of the bed, its grin widening as it pulled itself closer to Nia, who lay trembling beneath her soaked comforter.

"I am here for you," it whispered.

In her mind, Nia was still clinging to the last threads of hope, but her body was limp, her soul fraying. She would be lost, swallowed by a darkness no one would understand. To the world, she would be a headline. A tragedy. A mystery buried in a shallow grave.

"No..." she whimpered.

Kay-aR's grin split wider. "Poor little baby," it mocked. "There's nothing you can do. Your guardian is useless. He is a pitiful, sorry excuse for an angel. You are mine to possess. I haven't felt legs in so long, I can't wait to stand again."

It slithered onto the foot of the bed, its great weight pressing into the squeaky spring mattress, and its eyes twitching.

The closet door groaned, a sound so soft it could have been imagined. Kay-aR paused, and its head snapped toward the interruption.

"I'm already here," it muttered. "How can the closet… what is…?"

From the heart of the darkness, a pinprick of light bloomed. The light grew, pulsing outward, until the doorway was filled with a bright yellow light. A little girl stepped forward, no older than Nia, her cheeks round. Her skin glowed with a soft radiance.

"Hi, Kay-aR," she said. "I'm Daisy. I have a message for you… from Guardian. You remember her. The one who cut you in half."

Kay-aR's eyes bulged, its grin faltering. Its mouth opened… wider… and more still… revealing rows of glass-like teeth in a cavernous maw that is beyond the size of its head. Its tongue ignites into a ball of black flame that shoots toward Daisy like a comet, trailing smoke and ash.

Daisy raised a shimmering, liquid-gold shield, edged in silver and shaped like a diamond. The flame struck the shield and burst into white fire that dissolved into mist.

Daisy drew a long silver feather from behind her back. It shimmered and hardened into a sword, filling the room with a silvery holy light. She charged with the sword held high.

Kay-aR shrieked. "NOOO! Mine!"

Daisy's blade sliced through the air. It struck Kay-aR's head with a thunderous boom that shook the building to its foundation. Windows rattled, dust fell from the ceiling, and the sound rolled through the block like a shockwave.

In the master bedroom, Daisy felt Nia's parents bolt upright. Their hearts pounded so loud she almost covered her ears. "Nia!" they cried in unison.

The glowing girl observed them through the walls as they scrambled from their bed and collided in the hallway. Daisy stepped back to the wall beside the door. For a moment, the girl's mom could not grip the doorknob, so Dad pushed her aside. The door flew open, revealing their daughter lying still before them.

They gasped, breathless and confused, their minds racing faster than their bodies could keep up.

A soft, clear voice spoke behind them.

"Do not be afraid," Daisy said. "I'm here to help Nia. She's resting now, recovering from a great horror that has plagued her for a few days. The nightmares she told you about were real. She wasn't lying. She wasn't imagining, but she's safe now, and she needs rest."

The mother clutched her chest, her breath held after what she heard. Her knees gave way, and she slid down the wall, her mind spiraling. The strange boom, a child standing in her daughter's room, a monster in the closet, was real, and she never believed it.

Daisy felt the woman's thoughts, *I'm her mother. I was supposed to protect her. How could I not..."*

The father roared. "What is going on? Who are you? What are you doing in our home?"

Daisy turned, her expression calm but firm. "To make a long story short, I was sent by an Archangel. A demon was hunting Nia. A demon that preyed on torturing children. I know you think I'm crazy, I can see it on your faces. Don't worry, I'll be gone soon."

Their eyes drooped. Their bodies relaxed as they both stood before her. Their faces were blank as they returned to their room and fell into a deep sleep.

"All you'll remember," Daisy whispered, "is that the power transformer outside blew. That's what woke you."

She turned to Nia, brushing a damp curl from her forehead. "Sleep well, little one. Tomorrow will be a bright and glorious day for you. No fear. No terror. No monsters. Not for a while anyway."

To Thomas, who hovered in the corner, his glow returning. "You're free. No more chains against protecting her. Kay-aR was my responsibility. I'm sorry I was late."

Thomas smiled and faded into the shadows.

Daisy leaned close to Nia's ear. "I almost forgot the secret I was meant to tell you."

A tiny hole appeared at the top of Nia's ear as Daisy whispered into it. Nia smiles a little in her sleep.

Daisy kissed her forehead and stood. With a wave of her hand, the room was restored to normal. Every toy in its place, and all the blood and gore that trailed from the demon is gone, as if scrubbed away.

She walked to the closet, her form already fading.

"You're safe now," she said aloud. "Sleep well, little one."

Little Nia smiled, tears glistening in her eyes. Daisy stepped into the closet, and the door closed behind her with a gentle click.

IT IS TIME...

Long before the first breath of man stirred the dust, before time was measured by stars or sand, a secret was buried so deep within the Earth that even Hell had not found it, and most of Heaven had forgotten it. Long before Adam first stepped from Eden, a secret born of punishment was made.

Few still knew where the secret was kept. Father, Gabriel, Michael, and the single warden who had guarded the prison, who was unmoving, sleepless, and ever vigilant through every apocalypse or reset of Earth. Morningstar had once known, but even he could not recall where the prison was or who was in it after his failed rebellion. Not even the legions of Heaven nor the tormented hosts of Hell knew what slept beneath the crust of the world.

Till this day, the watcher stood guard. He was a rare angel, as most of his brothers had fallen over the millennia, either joining the rebellion against their Father or by teaching forbidden knowledge to humans and mating with them to create the abominations known as the Nephilim. Those who had interacted with the humans had been cursed and deformed, eventually dying in natural disasters guided by Father's hand.

This watcher was one of the last of the Grigori angels. He was a giant, but invisible to all but the Father, whom he only answered to. He stood in the valley, observing the prison gate. From time to time, humans camped and traveled across the massive gate, utterly unaware of what lay beneath or what stood over and watched them.

When anyone was nearby, he would tell Father, whether human, demon, or even angel, but he would not interact with them. A sentinel standing like a mountain for longer than time had been recorded. His orders were to remain unseen, but not because his proper form was terrible to behold. If others had discovered his post, they would have grown curious.

If he could have been seen, the light of Father radiated from him like a blinding star. His body was covered in eyes, allowing him to see all things. Even with his physical form hidden, his presence often instilled fear in those who lingered in the area for too long. He had stood by as myths and folktales were woven about the valley, claiming it was haunted by witches, shapeshifting skinwalkers, and other creatures that humans conjured in their vivid imaginations.

He cared not about humans or demons. His only focus was on the prison and the sinful prisoner that was held within.

The one whom almost all others had forgotten waited in a stone prison of eternal silence, its penance stretching across the millennia. The single occupant waited for the voice of Father to forgive.

This prisoner was once an Archangel honored above most others in the height of her grandness. Eya was her name.

Once, she had been a beloved teacher, a counselor, and a warrior of Heaven. Wings that shimmered with sunlight had wrapped her naked form, and her voice had soothed the trembling hearts of the newly created. By Michael's side, she was a devoted pupil and had earned the reverence of her peers through compassion.

However, compassion in war can often become a form of betrayal.

When the Great War erupted, as Lucifer was bloated with pride, he rallied those who could not stomach the elevation of man over the angels. Eya was called to fight. The Morningstar had convinced a third of the angels to help him destroy the piles of dirt that Father had favored over their power and beauty.

Michael had called all the loyal angels to join him and stop the fallen from destroying Father's favorite creation.

Eya was ordered to flank the rebels, to hem them in so that Michael could strike with his mighty sword, but she did not. Among the clouds above all the madness, her wings folded tight, her heart broke as the clash of steel and fury shattered the peace of Heaven. Tears fell as her brothers and sisters tore each other apart over the love Father had given to a creature of clay. She wept for Adam, who was unaware of the entire threat, for the angels, for the world that was unraveling.

Memories replayed in her mind to distract her from the deaths of her brothers and sisters as they fought. Adam was the most curious creation Father had ever made, and she laughed at this little frail thing and his joy in learning.

She had loved Adam the instant he had taken his first breath. He was a curiosity, and she loved him nearly as much as Father. The angels that despised him did not sit well with her. Their words were betrayal against Father, but she could never hate them or want to destroy them.

Fighting against her own family, even if it was Father's command to protect Adam, was impossible for a being that only wanted things to be peaceful again between her brethren.

The clouds did not hide the sounds of battle, with clashing armor, shields, and roars that shattered the once peaceful heavens. The war seemed to last forever to her, but in truth, it was over in the blink of an eye. When the war faded, she was summoned.

She came before Michael, bent and broken, her once radiant face streaked with tears. Her wings dragged behind her like wilted petals. Michael stood tall, his hand trembling as he raised it to cast her into Hell with the rest of the fallen.

Before judgment fell, a soft voice spoke.

"Hold thy judgment," it said. "Father has shown mercy because of the love that is in her heart. She shall pay her penance in prayer instead."

Gabriel descended beside her, his face wet. "You abandoned your duty," he said. "Many fell because of you, but you will be forgiven when Father wills it."

Michael lowered his arm, relief and grief mingling in his eyes, and turned to leave.

Gabriel placed his hand upon her brow. "You will be stripped of your title. Your Grace will be taken. You will be buried deep within the Earth, far from Heaven, far from Hell. You will suffer alone until Father calls your name again."

Eya rose, her eyes closed, her arms spread wide. She had earned this punishment.

Father whispered, "So shall it be, as you say, the punishment shall be handed." Even as gentle as the sound of his words was intended, his voice was as mighty as an exploding star. In the blink of an eye, she fell. Cast down from heaven towards a destination that was known only by Father and the faithful watcher that followed her.

She plummeted through the skies, her body limp, her wings torn away. The wind screamed around her, ripping her flesh, shredding her robes until she was bare and bleeding. Hair whipped like flame as her skin flayed by the descent.

The only noise she made was a prayer as her bones cracked and her skin split, as the air grew colder and thinner. She prayed for forgiveness, for redemption, for the grace she had lost.

The sky glowed, turning the night into a false dawn, brighter than any day had ever known.

What was left of her struck the Earth with such force that the world shuddered. A boom echoed across continents so deep it rattled the bones of mountains. Trees exploded into splinters. Valleys collapsed. Dust rose in a choking wave that blanketed half the globe.

Where she fell, a deep crater formed. Its depths are so deep that it swallowed light. It was not long before the earth around the crater fell in and buried the hole, creating the forgotten prison. The watcher stood at his post and made sure Eya remained, praying in her sleep for forgiveness that only a few beings even remembered she desired.

Time passed. Ice ages came and went. The continents shifted. The crater was flooded and then it eroded, but beneath it, buried in stone, Eya remained.

For ages, the Earth had flourished above a buried truth. Under root and stone, underneath the memory of time, a punishment slumbered. The angel was all but forgotten. The watcher was waiting.

On a night thick with rain, the world stirred. A voice whispered across the universe to the land the Grigori stood over: "It is time."

To the watcher, the sound was like the warmth of the sun, but if any of the humans had heard it, they would have burned to ash in an instant. The voice of Father was an eternal flame of purity that no human could withstand anymore. Humans had fallen so far since the days of Adam, but the watcher did not care about that. His job was done, and now he was no longer required to observe the prison.

The valley, untouched by man's inventions, shuddered as thunder cracked across the sky. A bolt of lightning tore the heavens in two, illuminating the drenched terrain with a blinding light that made each raindrop appear as a falling star. The storm raged, and the air was so dense with electricity that it made even the watcher's skin crawl. The clouds churned, and the mountains trembled.

The ground buckled and heaved, as if the Earth itself were trying to reject what was about to rise. The final boom echoed deeper than thunder. The silence that followed was so complete it felt like the world had stopped breathing.

Defiant, a bolt of lightning struck the valley floor with such force that the ground rippled. Debris exploded outward, the fragments turned to dust midair, drifting in glowing motes.

The storm faded and night returned, but only for a moment. The sun pierced the horizon, golden and sudden, as if impatient to witness what came next. Birds began to sing with jubilant abandon. Their songs rang through the trees, echoed by the rustle of small creatures emerging from burrows and nests. The forest came alive.

Gradually, the beasts calmed and became silent. The wildlife turned their eyes skyward, sensing something was amiss. A soft white light radiated above the valley, casting long shadows that danced under the trees.

From nowhere and everywhere, a voice spoke, gentle as a breeze, but as fierce as the sun.

"Eya, you are forgiven."

The light descended, folding into itself, and the animals turned their gaze to a patch of earth. The soil trembled as if a volcano were about to erupt. The ground bulged, cracked, and split as a hand emerged, pale and trembling, its fingers splayed.

The hand paused before another burst forth, clenched in a fist. The ground erupted, sending a spray of dirt and stone into the air, but the debris dissolved into dust before it could touch the creatures watching. They did not flinch or flee.

From the crater, a feminine figure rose. The human-shaped being was covered in soil and shards of obsidian. She sat in silence, her breath slow, her eyes closed. Around her, the forest leaned in. Birds resumed their song. The wind carried the scent of wet earth and blooming moss. She inhaled, filling her lungs. A smile stretched across the dirt-stained face.

Tears carved clean paths on her filthy cheeks as she tilted her face to the sky. "Father," she whispered, "thank you. I will not fail you again. I will find her, the one I am to help."

From the clear sky, rain began to fall. The drops were warm, gentle, and fragrant with the petals of many flowers. The downpour washed over Eya, rinsing away the centuries of dust and shame. She spun, letting the water cleanse her from scalp to heel. The cleaned skin glowed beneath it, reborn.

When the rain ceased, a cold wind swirled around her. The woman opened her eyes as the wind died and looked at her bare form. A smile stretched across her face with a tilt of her head as she noticed the small creatures all around her.

"Will you help me?" she asked.

Leaves and bushes rustled. From the undergrowth, three turtles emerged, their shells glistening with dew. Upon their backs rode spiders and caterpillars. Each bug was vibrant and strange.

The turtles plodded towards her, and their mouths were turned upward almost as if they were smiling, as they reached her toes. The insects dismounted, crawling onto her feet, their tiny legs tickling her skin and forcing her to giggle.

The spiders and caterpillars climbed her legs and began their work. Silk unfurled from their bodies, shimmering blue. They marched in patterns, weaving all around her. Their abdomens contracted in a synchronized rhythm.

The woman closed her eyes, lifted her chin to feel the sun on her face, and stood still as the creatures clothed her. The spiders swung from her to weave a sheer gown of light blue. The caterpillars continued upwards along her midsection to wrap her in more silk.

As she stood still, embracing the tickle of so many tiny hairy legs circling her, she felt the silk stretch and expand to fill in the sheerness of her undergarments until she was decent.

In an instant, she wore a soft, short gown that clung to her strong body, glowing with a quiet yet powerful blue radiance. She looked down, touched the fabric, and smiled.

"Thank you, my little friends."

The insects paused as if to say, "*You're welcome*," and returned to the turtles. The turtles turned and vanished into the forest, leaves parting to let them pass.

To the gathered animals, her voice was warm and gentle. "I will be leaving now. Thank you for making my return a blessed one."

She faced the sun, her gown catching the fiery light.

"I am coming to help you, little Nia."

With that, she walked into the dawn.

NEXT STORY

The moment Eya whispered, "I am coming, Nia," the world seemed to pause for the watcher just long enough for another ancient to stir and draw his attention. It had been an eternity since he had bothered to look beyond the prison of Eya, and now it was no more. No further command came from father, and so the Grigori did what he does; he continued to watch.

From the depths of a cavern carved by suffering, a voice gurgled up through the blackness. It sounded as though it were speaking through thick water, each syllable bloated and distorted.

"Ssi amzz coommming llllittle NNNiaaahhhh…"

The echo rolled through the chamber, bouncing off walls slick with flesh and bone. A pool of darkness, twelve feet in width, was perfectly still. The surface rippled before it exploded outward in a geyser of black sludge and bone fragments. Before the debris could fall to the floor, it reversed and sucked back into the place it began.

Instead of returning as a pool of inky black, the mass coalesced into a towering figure, its body forged from the darkness from which it emerged. The sludge clung to it, absorbing into its form with a sickening hiss, as if it were rain vanishing into cracked desert soil.

The creature spread its limbs wide, its joints cracking. The laugh that erupted from it was a deep, guttural sound that vibrated the air and caused the walls to tremble.

"Ssi amzz coommming llllittle NNNiaaahhhh…"

The watcher remained unseen as he drifted into the cavern and observed. Unlike the archangels and other angels, the Grigori were tied to all the realms of mortals and demons as much as the heavens. There was no boundary they could not cross, but their sole job was to observe and report to Father, and so he did.

The towering demon turned toward a fleshy wall, unaware of the observing visitor. The surface was slick and veined, and the demon began to claw at it. Its talons tore through the flesh, peeling it in bloody strips. The wall was a living tapestry of charred human remains. Bones jutted at odd angles, some still wrapped in twitching sinew. Others were fresh, still steaming, their owners not yet dead.

Black-red fire danced across the surface, moving like a sentient thing. The flames slithered up and down the walls, caressing the flesh. Wherever it touched, the tissue spasmed and melted. Screams echoed from within the walls, some human, some not.

The floor was no better. The ground vibrated beneath the creature's feet, made of the same meaty substance, riddled with embedded skulls and shattered ribs. In the center of the chamber, a pool churned with a thick, viscous plasma, the color of old blood and bile. Bubbles popped on the surface as if stirred by unseen hands.

Chunks of flesh floated on the surface. Some were limbs. Others were half-devoured torsos. Most were small and infant sized. Their skin was torn, their bones gnawed. Bite marks and claw slashes covered every inch.

From the edges of the pool, malformed claws reached, grasping at the meat. One snagged a chunk and pulled it under.

Amid the random moans from the walls, a child's scream pierced the air.

A skeletal arm burst from the liquid, fingers twitching as if testing the air. Another followed. Then a third. They remained suspended in the air before bending down to the edges of the pool and lifting. From between the arms, a head emerged.

The face was half-bitten, its scalp was peeled, revealing writhing tissue beneath. Its eyes were set asymmetrical, with one bulging and the other sunken. There was no nose, no ears. Its mouth was oversized, filled with jagged, blackened teeth. Beneath its skin, something wiggled around under its skin.

A blister swelled above its lip and burst. Green pus sprayed outward, and from the wound crawled a worm with a gaping maw. The worm partially slipped out as clumps of pus fell from the gaping hole. The parasite wiggled around the lip, never entirely leaving the wound as if it were part of the same flesh.

The creature rose, its skin ripped and clinging to its body, revealing the twisted skeleton and muscle underneath. It twisted, its limbs bending in ways that defied the laws of anatomy. Its feet were broken, clawed stumps that touched the ground with a wet, slapping sound.

The new demon stood hunched, listening to the screams of the few bodies in the walls and floor that still breathed.

The shriek that erupted from it shattered the air, silencing the flames, the screams, and the tearing of the meat. The cavern itself seemed to recoil, expanding and contracting as if the air itself had flinched. The towering demon that had been tearing at the walls melted into a pit of black ooze as if to hide.

The creature raised its arms, and its voice thundered through the open space even though its mouth did not move.

"Where is the flesh of the children I love to eat? So sweet when fresh... so full of rancid innocence. I grow weary. I have feasted on many souls, but now I crave the final course. Little Nia... my dessert. Where is she?"

The body erupted in flames, licking at the walls and igniting the air around it. The cavern trembled and flickered in and out of existence as if reality itself were unsure whether to hold or collapse.

The creature stood still, waiting and listening for the answer. As the flames died, its cracked and burned skin softened into the hanging flesh it had been.

In a flash, a black and red ball of swirling flame appeared, hovering before it. The air filled with the sound of tearing meat, and from the fire, a voice emerged, resembling the sound of ripping flesh but somehow forming words.

"Nia yet lives. Eya, the former right hand of the Archangel Michael, is seeking her."

The air in the cavern sucked away for a moment, creating a vacuum. It returned with a blast that caused the fleshy walls to expand, ripping and spilling blood to the soft floor.

"Nooooo! I will not be denied! I will feast on her flesh! Michael! You broke your word! Michael! You swore no Angel or Archangel would interfere! I demand an audience. I was promised the girl. Bring me the girl now!"

A pinpoint of light grew before the demon. The radiance expanded into a gaseous, half-formed humanoid shape.

A calm and clear voice spoke. "Michael sends me. He

did not break his word. No Angel in Heaven or on Earth has interfered as was his promise, but you... You broke yours. You tried to kill Nia when she was younger. You sent your demon to possess her and take her before it was time."

The creature snarled. "Then why is Eya here? She is an Archangel!"

The humanoid replied, "Eya was not in Heaven. Nor on Earth. She was under the Earth. Buried. Forgotten. The terms did not bind her. Michael's word holds. Yours does not."

Flesh cracked as the demon trembled. The remaining flames across its twisted body sputtered and vanished.

The voice faded, and with it, the light dissolved into the ether. It lunged at the vanishing glow, its claws slicing through empty air. It tensed like a coiled spring and released a roar that fractured the fabric of the space around it.

Black and blue flames erupted from its core, devouring all in their path. The walls, once slick with flesh and bone, collapsed inward, imploding as if sucked into a void. Time itself shattered as the creature phased out of reality in a blur of shrieking distortion.

The watcher was ejected back into the valley where he once guarded Eya. He still received no new post, and so he followed the essence of the demon across the Earth to a quiet place with fields of crops and cows.

In a quiet farmhouse tucked deep in the countryside, a young woman lay asleep. She was bare and warm beneath soft sheets. A smile was on her face, her breath slow, her skin glowing with the flush of mythical touch in her dreams. The scent of lavender lingered in the air, mingling with the faint musk of her own skin.

2:59:50 a.m.

Dreams of her lover's fingers tracing golden

shoulders, with lips brushing against her sun-kissed flesh. Her husband would never know.

2:59:55 a.m.

A beautiful, flirty smile. A sigh. A soft moan as the lips of the woman and her lover pressed together, lost in the hush of the night.

3:00:00 a.m.

The woman's body convulsed, arching as a scream tore from her throat. Eyes snapped open, wild and searching, but no answer came. Pain grew behind her ribs and spread like wildfire. Her spine cracked with a sickening pop, her teeth ground so hard they shattered, fragments bursting from her mouth in a spray of blood and enamel.

Her chest swelled as the fluids of life surged beneath it. The woman reached for her solar plexus, but her limbs were yanked backward and pinned by an invisible force. Eyes bulged, veins burst and exploded. Hot fluid streamed down her cheeks as blood geysered from her nose.

Her throat ruptured, spewing crimson foam and chunks of tissue. The scream she tried to release drowned in a flood of crimson, reduced to gurgling bubbles that hissed against her lips. The belly trembled, bloated with pressure, as the split from the throat opened in a jagged line that tore through to her navel.

From the ruin of her chest, thick talons emerged, glistening with viscous black fluid. They scraped against bones, tearing through muscle, grasping for escape. The woman, once beautiful, was now a mangled gateway, twitching with the last remnants of life.

The claws belonged to a raw, meaty arm, wrapped in scorched flesh that peeled like old bark. The hand rose, dripping with hot, syrupy blood that steamed in the cool air.

The woman's body gave way as black flames burst from the gaping hole. Thick smoke spewed from the fire across the floor around the room.

What was left of her collapsed in a heap of loose flesh and bones. From the carnage, laughter emanated from the wound as a creature emerged that was massive and hunched. Creamy blood dripped from its ruined flesh. The demon was far larger than the woman; as it squeezed through the gateway it had made of her, it entered the Earth in physical form.

The demon seized her arm, sinking its talons deep into the meat, and brought it to its mouth. Its jaws were a ruin of shattered, jagged, black teeth. A split tongue slithered out, probing the meat, tasting it. The monster giggled, the same sound that had been from deep within the corpse it had just vacated.

Tossing the arm aside, it reached around its back and grabbed her head. The woman's face, still warm, was lifted to its own burned, misshapen head. The demon whispered in a voice thick with mucus and malice:

"I have feasted on your soul, your flesh… now I will devour your face. I do hope it is delicious."

Its tongue burrowed into her eye socket, followed by its teeth, which sank into the soft tissue with a wet crunch. It wrapped its cracked lips around the socket and sucked, slurping loudly as the contents of her skull were drained.

When it finished, it pulled the skull away, lazily withdrawing its tongue. The demon tossed the hollow head aside and smiled. It laughed again, but this time, the voice changed.

The wet, gravelly growl softened and became melodic. A woman's voice that was sweet, lilting, and beautiful rose from the monster's throat like a songbird's tune.

Its body began to change, and the transformation was

grotesque. The raw meat rippled, bones snapping into new places, flesh smoothing over exposed muscle. Hair sprouted long, black, and glossy. Breasts formed, hips curved, and skin darkened to a golden tan.

The demon stood nude amid the blood and torn flesh. Her full lips pursed, her eyes impossibly blue, her figure flawless. She was an echo of the woman she had just consumed.

She licked her fingers, her lips, her arms, cleaning herself with feral delight. The new smile was radiant, but the hunger in her eyes betrayed the monster beneath.

A roar escaped her as she threw her head back. A sound so powerful it cracked the walls, shattered windows, and sent shockwaves through the countryside. Trees bent. Cars flipped. Power lines snapped. The earth trembled beneath her fury.

Once she was done, she stood in the center of the destruction, laughing. The growly cackling echoed across the hills. She walked through the debris, her bare feet leaving bloody prints in the dust. The sun rose, casting golden light across her skin.

Staring into the blinding orb, she whispered, "Here I come to eat your flesh, little Nia."

The radio crackled to life at 6:00 a.m., its speakers humming with static before the song began. A sultry voice spilled into the room, syrupy and slow.

"Welcome to my imagination... let me inside that beautiful mind of yours... so I can play with you... kiss your thoughts... sleep with your soul forever..."

The melody slithered through the air, wrapping around the bed. Nia stirred beneath the covers in a tangled heap of limbs and linen. Her hand emerged, pale and drowsy, and slapped the alarm clock with a dull thud. It tumbled to the floor, clattering against the hardwood.

"Coffee," she mumbled, voice hoarse and half-dreaming.

The pile on the bed shifted, rising like a creature shedding its cocoon. Blankets slid to the floor in a soft cascade, revealing a mop of tangled hair that trailed down the girl's head. She shuffled toward the bathroom, a shambling silhouette of sleep, muttering again, "Coffee..."

Steam curled from the bathroom door an hour later. Nia emerged transformed with her skin dewy, her eyes bright, and her hair cascading in glossy waves. She moved with the grace of someone reborn, but her voice remained unchanged.

"Coffee."

Nia glided into the kitchen, drawn to the pot like a moth to flame. The scent of brewing grounds filled the air, rich, earthy, and comforting. She reached for her favorite mug. The one with Marilyn Monroe, featuring the iconic white dress that was lifted by a gust of wind. Her fingers curled around the ceramic, eyes never leaving the pot as it hissed and sputtered its final breath.

The daily ritual was complete. Those magic beans were the best discovery she ever made.

Moments later, she sat at the table, the mug warm in her hands. The smell of bacon and eggs, which her mother had left before going to work, mingled with the steam of coffee as she sat down to breakfast. Outside, the morning light filtered through the blinds in golden slats.

A jolt of pain stabbed through her skull that was sharp, electric, and primal. Her vision blurred and her hands trembled. The mug slipped from her grasp and shattered against the floor, coffee splashing across her bare feet.

Her voice cracked the air as she screamed. She clutched her head, nails digging into her scalp, as images flooded her mind of burning cities, torn bodies, rivers of blood. The windows shuddered and cracked, as if the house itself recoiled from her agony.

"God, help me!" she cried.

In an instant, the room fell quiet. The pain vanished. The tremors ceased. The kitchen quieted, save for the faint drip of coffee pooling beneath the table.

Nia opened her eyes, heart pounding. Her skin was clammy, her muscles taut. She pressed herself against the nearest wall, scanning the room for threats. A trembling rippled through her. She slid to the floor, knees drawn to her chest, trying not to pass out as her breath came in shallow gasps.

A soft, warm breeze blew past her and brushed against her cheek, carrying a floral scent unlike anything she had ever known. Her muscles relaxed as her heartbeat slowed. A whisper was in her ear, soft as silk.

"I am Guardian. I am an Angel sent to deliver a message. Little Nia, an ancient Archangel more powerful than you can imagine, is coming to help you."

Nia blinked, dazed. "Who are you? Who is Guardian?"

The voice thundered, shaking the air.

"I am here to inform you that your life will change forever!"

The force of it almost knocked her back, but she held firm, her willpower stronger than her fear. She gritted her teeth and asked again, louder this time.

"Who are you? Who is Guardian?"

The words softened, becoming tender.

"Child, I am a herald. I am here to announce the

arrival of Eya, the right hand of Michael. She has been in penance since before Eden was planted. Forgotten by most of Heaven. Unknown to most in Hell. She is coming to train you."

Nia's mind reeled. Her voice was barely a whisper. "W-why me?"

The herald replied, "You come from a bloodline of warriors. A master demon hungers for you. He will feast on you and all who stand in his way."

Nia curled into a trembling ball. "This is insane. I'm dreaming. I must be crazy. I'm having a nightmare. Wake up, Nia. Wake up!"

"Little Nia, fear not. Eya will protect you. I must go, but you must choose if you will become her champion. Think it over. Be blessed."

Nia lay still in the silence that followed. She took a deep breath, her throat dry, her thoughts hazy. Somehow, she had always felt different. She had always worked harder, pushed further, reached higher.

Now she understood why she had always felt blessed, even though nothing ever came easy.

She stood, legs shaky, and walked to the bathroom. As she reached the hallway, she felt that her body was changing. Seeing herself in the mirror, eyes bulging and heart thudding strong enough to see her shirt vibrate.

The choice of a more difficult life as a warrior of God on Earth was now hers to make. As she sat on the cold plastic seat and listened to the stream dribble below her, she wondered why and how a twelve-year-old girl could ever protect the world from demons.

With her first wipe, she discovered another revelation for the morning. She leaned over and grabbed her mother's box of feminine hygiene products. Nia was now a woman. Was this strange feeling in the kitchen some part of this?

Later, she returned to the kitchen, finished her breakfast, and poured fresh coffee into her travel mug. After sweeping up the shards of her favorite mug, she dumped them in a container to rinse and glue together later. She slung her backpack over one shoulder and stepped outside.

The door clicked shut behind her. Her eyes glazed over, her voice distant.

"I go forth toward the light."

She blinked, shook her head. "Wow. That was weird." And with that, she walked toward school. Toward destiny.

Moments after the sun cast its first golden fingers across the rooftops, a woman appeared at the edge of Nia's driveway. She did not arrive by car, nor did her footsteps echo with the crunch of gravel. The strangely tall woman was standing there as if the morning had conjured her from mist.

The dress she wore shimmered, catching the light in rippling waves of silver and blue. It clung to her form with a fluid grace, swaying gently. Hair, long and black as midnight, spilled down her back in thick, glossy strands. Despite her height and the defined muscles, her movements were delicate, with each bare footstep measured and each gesture soft, as if she feared disturbing something fragile beneath the surface of the world.

The woman approached the front door, her eyes tracing the wood grain as if reading a story etched into its surface. A faint warm glow radiated from her face. She placed her hand on the door, fingers splayed, and closed her eyes.

"I am here for you, Nia. This is where we begin. For now, all who enter shall be protected from evil... but not from life."

She lowered herself onto the top step, her dress pooling around her. Her gaze drifted to the grass, the trees, the windless morning. The air was unnaturally still, the birds silent, the leaves unmoving.

"I need your help, little ones," she said.

At first, nothing stirred. Then, the grass rippled. A swarm of ants emerged. Beetles followed, their shells iridescent. Bees buzzed low, their wings vibrating with a strange rhythm, and birds descended from the branches above, landing on her lap and shoulders.

"Do you know who Nia is?" she asked with a smile.

The creatures did not speak, but they shifted, twitched, and fluttered as if nodding in unison. The light in her eyes flared once and faded, as her smile deepened.

"Good. I need your help protecting her. Watch over her until I return. If she is in unnatural danger, you must tell me."

She paused, listening to the rustle of wings, the click of mandibles, the soft chirps and whispers.

"Thank you," she said.

The insects retreated, disappearing into the grass and leaves. The birds lifted off, vanishing into the canopy. The bees hovered for a moment before they zipped away.

Her toes touched the earth as she rose from the steps, and she turned toward the sidewalk. As she walked, the shadows seemed to stretch toward her, as if reluctant to let her go.

"I will return this afternoon," she said. "She must choose to let me help her destroy the evil or let it devour her."

She paused at the side of the street, her silhouette framed by the rising sun.

"But I have faith," she whispered. "She will choose to walk in the light. Now I must find her."

She vanished down the road, her dress trailing behind her.

The classroom was filled with concentrating students, the scratch of pencils, and the dull hum of fluorescent lights. Nia sat by the window, her math book open, her fingers curled around a mechanical pencil. The numbers blurred as she leaned in, trying to focus.

Tap, tap, tap.

The sound was so faint it could have been imagined.

Tap. Tap.

She blinked, her gaze drifting to the glass. A hummingbird hovered there, its wings a blur of iridescent green and violet, tapping its beak against the pane. The sound was so soft it barely pierced through the sounds of turning pages and the scribbling around the classroom.

Nia tilted her head. The bird paused mid-air, darted upward, looped, and returned, fluttering in a strange, rhythmic dance. She smiled, and the bird seemed to respond, its movements growing more animated, almost theatrical, but something was off.

Her vision narrowed. The edges of the room faded, the sounds dulled as if she had tunnel vision. She blinked hard, rubbed her eyes. "Wow," she whispered. "I must really be tired."

Nia looked again. The bird was still now, perched on the ledge, staring at her. Its tiny head tilted once and then again, more deliberately. If she had not known any better, she would have thought it was a nod.

"Hello, little one," she murmured. "Are you here to help me?"

Another nod. This time, it was unmistakable.

She leaned closer to the glass. "Come to me during lunch. I'll be on the bench near the tree with the pink flowers."

The hummingbird hovered for a moment and darted away. For a while, she wondered if she had been daydreaming.

Nia returned to her studies, but her thoughts were elsewhere. The strange morning events a home, and now a hummingbird, played through her head like a movie.

When the lunch bell rang, she kept a brisk pace. The locker clanged shut, and her lunch bag was cool against her palm. The hallway smelled of cafeteria grease and pencil shavings. She pushed through the doors into the sunlight.

The hummingbird descended in a blur, hovered before her face, and landed on her shoulder. Its tiny claws pricked against her skin through her shirt. Nia smiled and walked toward the bench.

A tree loomed over the bench, its blossoms dancing in the light breeze. The air grew still and heavy with the scent of jasmine.

"Hello," she called. "Where are you?"

A voice answered, soft and melodic from behind her. "I am right behind this beautiful tree."

A tall, regal woman stepped into view. Her dress shimmered, and her black hair flowed over her shoulders. She was barefoot, her feet dusted with soil but unmarred, as if the earth itself refused to harm her.

"Hello, little Nia," she said. "Though I suppose 'little' no longer fits. Let me introduce myself…"

Nia's eyes widened. "Your name is Eya, you were sent to help me, and you've traveled a long way."

Eya's smile deepened. "Yes."

She stepped closer, and the air around her shimmered. "A Master demon is coming. It wants you, your body and soul to gain strength and power. It thought you were unprotected, but I am here, and you… You knew I was coming. How?"

Nia's voice was steady. "I think I've always known. Since I was small. I've felt different. Like something inside me was waiting. I want this. I want to help. I might be twelve, but I feel like I've lived a very long time. I've always wanted to help people, and I was somehow destined to be special in some way that nobody understood."

The woman inhaled, her expression unreadable. "You understand more than I expected. That says much about who you are."

Nia sat on the bench, the hummingbird still perched on her shoulder. "I'm ready to learn more. I've got forty-five minutes."

Eya spoke as fast as Nia could understand, her words weaving a tapestry of ancient truths and threats. She listened, her lunch untouched, her fingers gripping the bench.

"So, I'm to be a warrior," she said. "To fight demons. To protect others and destroy unholy things. This is a lot to take in."

"Yes," Eya said. "But even if you choose not to, the demon still comes. You must decide."

Nia nodded. "Meet me at my house. Eight o'clock."

Eya turned, her dress catching the light. She walked away, her bare feet silent on the grass.

Nia returned to school, the hummingbird lifting off her shoulder just before she stepped inside. The hallway felt colder now, the fluorescent lights harsher. She moved through the day as if a ghost, but beneath her calm exterior, her thoughts were a hurricane.

When the final bell rang, she gathered her things and left through the entrance. Each step felt heavier, as if the ground itself resisted her. At the last step outside, she paused, thinking about her life moving forward. Would school even matter?

A flutter brushed her ear. The hummingbird landed again, and this time it was not alone. She smiled at the bird. "Well, little one, I guess you and I are going to be besties."

A butterfly settled on her wrist. A bee on her shoulder. A moth on her hair. More tiny, winged companions clung to her, covering her as living ornaments.

"I guess I have a bunch of friends."

Students standing nearby in a circle looked at her as if she were a weirdo. Phones clicked as they took pictures. She did not care.

"If you print them out," she said, "I'll autograph them."

She walked home with a spring in her step, the insects clinging to her. The moment she reached her door, they lifted off, swirling around her in a spiral of color and sound.

They flew over the house. Nia pondered where they were headed when she heard a chorus of birds singing. She followed the sound around the home to the gate leading into the backyard. The birdsong was clearer, and the music called to her.

Nia reached for the gate's latch as the ground at her feet moved. A trail of ants marched in perfect formation to form a heart.

Within the center, spiders spun in slow circles with their legs brushing against one another in a synchronized ritual. Their bodies glowed with a faint iridescence, as if lit from within.

She knelt and reached toward them.

"Hello there, little ones," she whispered. "Are you my friends too?"

The spiders paused mid-spin. The ants halted. One by one, they climbed onto Nia's outstretched finger, their tiny legs tickling her skin. She smiled, her eyes wide with wonder.

With her free hand, she unlatched the gate and stepped into the backyard. As she turned the corner, the backyard burst into motion.

Birds swooped in spirals overhead, their colored feathers catching the rays from the lowering sun. Squirrels darted through the branches, tails flicking. Rabbits emerged from the underbrush, their noses twitching, and a fox spied from the shadows.

In the center of it all sat Eya. The tall woman was cross-legged on the grass, her dress pooling around her. Her hair spilled over her shoulders in waves of black silk. The animals danced around her, drawn to her presence.

Eya looked up, and her eyes were glowing.

"Okay, friends," she said. "I need to speak with Nia. Please give us space."

The creatures scattered, their wings beating, limbs skittering, and tails whipping as they fled into the trees and melted into the darkness.

Nia lowered her arm, letting the spiders and ants crawl off. As the last ant reached her hand, it turned and seemed to nod.

"Goodbye for now. I'll see you later."

The girl turned to Eya. "Can you sit? You're a little taller than I'm used to."

The tall woman chuckled and settled onto the grass. Nia sat across from her, knees nearly touching. The ground beneath them felt warm.

Eya's gaze was steady. "We didn't get to talk about me much earlier. Do you know who I am? And what you are?"

Nia hesitated. "Not exactly, but I think you're here to help me understand. I know your name, and I believe you're here to help me discover my true self."

"I am an Archangel," Eya said. "Sent to lead you to your destiny."

Nia stared, her eyes searching Eya's face with aching recognition as if she had always known, somewhere deep in her bones.

Eya smiled. "I've come too far through time and distance to hold back."

The archangel reached into the earth, her fingers sinking deep into the soil. She lifted a handful of dirt, holding it between them, and let it fall through her fingers.

The breeze caught it, swirling it around Nia in a soft spiral. As the last grain touched her skin, her vision blurred into a haze.

The image of a girl named Daisy flashed through her mind, along with the demon that had tormented her youth. She saw Eya's fall, her penance, and her rise again. She even felt another presence standing watch when Eya rose, but it was gone a moment later, pursuing something else now.

The images flickered behind her eyes, and when the haze lifted, she gasped. She blinked a few times to clear her vision.

"You... you're an Archangel. A true Archangel."

Eya leaned forward. "Are you alright?"

"I've always felt different. Not just growing up, not

just the changes of becoming a woman with the pimples and all. I've felt... watched over. Protected."

"You were. Your guardian loves you deeply. He still checks in from time to time. A little birdy told me he's so proud of who you've become."

Nia's voice cracked. "Tell him thank you. He did a great job, considering the rough and tumble childhood I led."

"You're not afraid in any way, or frightened of what I am?"

"No," Nia said. "I've felt a holy presence my whole life. I think I was meant for something more."

Eya's expression grew solemn. "If you choose this path, your training will be brutal. You'll face horrors no child should, but you'll become a warrior unlike any before. Even Adam Monroe, who defended against evil for several years. He has stepped aside to raise a new family. You may meet him one day, but for now, you must understand this fight is yours. I cannot defeat the demon. Only you can. Do you truly understand what could happen to you?"

Nia's eyes darkened. "I understand. I may be twelve, but I know what's at stake."

Eya nodded and plunged her hand into the earth again, deeper this time, all the way to her wrist. She twisted, the soil groaning around her arm as if she was mixing cake batter, and whispered with a smile, "Thank you."

She pulled slowly, and from the ground emerged a thick, gnarled root. It stretched as she rose, growing longer and heavier until it reached a length of five feet. With a final tug, it snapped free.

Eya held it in both hands, closed her eyes, and murmured, "With all the grace of Heaven, I give this staff to Nia, to aid her in any way she needs in the battles to come."

She extended it to the girl, and Nia reached out.

The moment her fingers touched the wood, warmth surged through her with a golden hum that filled her veins, her lungs, her bones. She gasped, her skin tingling, her heart racing.

Nia gripped the wood with both hands, and the energy intensified, wrapping around her like armor. She lowered one end to the ground.

A gust of wind exploded outward from the point that touched the earth, lifting her hair, clothes, and spirit. The world roared around her and quickly fell silent.

Eya smiled. "The earth is pleased. The tree that gave this root is honored to be part of your crusade."

Nia looked at the staff and up at Eya. "Tell her thank you."

The archangel extended her hand, her fingers glowing with a soft, golden light. Nia's hand was trembling from the gravity of what she was about to undertake.

"Let us begin," the archangel said, her voice steady. "Sit still. Close your eyes. You will travel to the land of Un. It is not a place of evil, but of sorrow. It will weigh heavy on your heart. There, you will learn to fight what claws at the soul."

Nia nodded, her eyes fluttering closed. "My soul is ready."

The air around her thickened. Her breath slowed, and her skin tingled.

In her mind, she was pulled forward, through a tunnel of light and shadow, until the world melted away. Nia now stood in a barren expanse.

The sky above was colorless, a pale smear of gray that offered no warmth. The ground beneath Nia's feet was dry and cracked, its surface resembling brittle parchment. A cold wind whispered across the land.

All around her drifted wisps of humanity, translucent and slow-moving. Their forms were smokey whisps, their faces blurred, and their eyes hollow. They sluggishly moved, as if weighed by centuries of grief.

Nia's chest tightened. The sorrow here was quiet, insidious, as a song played too softly to hear but impossible to ignore.

With her arms raised, her voice trembled but remained clear. "Father, these lost souls seek healing. Let them find the strength to take the first step toward you."

She turned to the drifting souls. "In the name of the Father, He is your savior. He is the way to healing."

Some of the figures paused. Their heads tilted. A few faded as mist would when it is caught in the sunlight. Others resumed their wandering, unchanged.

Nia lowered her arms. "They don't feel loved," she whispered. "But they are. I have faith that one day they will be saved."

She closed her eyes as the weight of the land pressed against her chest and was lifted. The sorrow peeled away as she was pulled back.

Returning to herself, she gasped and her body jolted upright. The air around her was warm again, filled with the scent of grass and wildflowers. She bowed her head, whispering a prayer for the souls still lost.

"Amen."

Eya's voice was soft but firm. "You now carry your greatest weapon, faith and love."

Nia opened her eyes. "No combat training? No punching or kicking?"

Eya smiled. "Faith in the Father and love for all creation is the greatest strength any human could have. With Heaven behind you, what force could stand against you?"

They shared a smile, and for a moment, Nia felt

whole, as if a final puzzle piece had fallen into place. Evil does not just attack the body. It devours the soul.

As the wind stirred to life around them, they stood. From the trees, the hummingbird returned, its wings a blur of iridescent light. Behind it came a procession of bees, butterflies, moths, and crawling things. Ants swarmed Eya's feet, forming intricate spirals. Spiders climbed her robes, their legs tickling her skin.

Two scorpions emerged from the underbrush, their black carapaces gleaming, their pincers snapping. They marched, stopping at Eya's feet.

The archangel looked at the pair. "You've come far. You understand what's needed?"

The scorpions bobbed once and vanished into the grass.

Eya stared after them. "They're strong. They came from where I was. They'll fight with you. Call them Kana and Nox, and they will understand you."

Nia nodded, her fingers tightening around the staff she now carried.

Eya turned toward the house. "They'll return soon, but for now, we have work to do."

As the watcher continued to follow the demon that was wrapped in the woman's visage, he sensed another disturbance near the town they were heading towards.

At midnight, beneath a sky smeared with ashy clouds and moonlight, the mausoleum at the edge of town exhaled a breath it had held for decades. The ancient cemetery surrounding it was filled with cracked

112

headstones. The trees were gnarled and leafless, and their branches were skeletal fingers.

Inside the mausoleum, the air was heavy with mildew and the sour tang of old stone. A single marble coffin lay in the center, its surface slick with dew from the humidity that clung to everything. The man inside had died violently as his body had shattered against a roadside pole when he lost control of his Porsche and flew through his windshield. His soul was already blackened long before the crash.

There were three women buried on a wooded property that the man once owned. They had never been found. He had taken their lives after trapping them for his own sinful pleasures. He had discarded them in a sinkhole. In his will, he instructed that the hole be filled with cement and dirt to protect people from falling in.

No mourners had come to visit him, no one had shown up at his funeral other than his attorney, who had hated him. No prayers had been whispered. His millions, begrudgingly left to charity, had done more goodness in death than he ever had in life; his attorney had made sure of that.

The dew on the sarcophagus began to steam, curling upward in thin tendrils. From the seams of the lid, black smoke seeped out, slow at first, then thick and choking. The fumes smelled of scorched hair.

A crack split the stone with a bone-cracking noise.

Dark red fire burst forth, like blood forced through a ruptured artery. The flames surged outward, engulfing the mausoleum in a sphere of hellfire. The stone walls blackened, and the air filled with inhuman screams. The fire consumed the surface, and the stone melted into nothing.

The mausoleum collapsed inward, reduced to rubble, and from the center of the ruin, a figure rose.

He stood naked, his skin flawless, his form that of a middle-aged man. Too perfect. Too still. His eyes glowed with a light that had never touched Heaven. His smile was inhumanly long, his teeth too sharp, and his breath steamed in the cold air.

He raised his arms, his voice echoing a hymn twisted by madness.

"Come to me, all. Come to your master and serve me as I command."

From the soil all around the cemetery, a thin, pale mist began to rise, screaming. One soul. Then another. Then dozens. They drifted upward, their forms barely human, their mouths open in eternal agony. These were the damned, the murderers, the predators, the ones who had earned Hell's embrace. They had learned too late what salvation meant.

Now, they were fuel. Hell was never concerned with genders or fancy titles. All were welcome.

The mists floated toward him, an obsession that promised only pain. As they entered his flesh, the demon shuddered, his body rippling as if it might burst at any moment. His head snapped back with a roar so violent that it shattered headstones, cracked crypts, and sent car alarms wailing two miles away.

Buildings trembled. Windows fractured. Dogs howled.

He laughed, the sound wet and guttural.

"I can smell you, Nia," he hissed. "And that weak little Angel, but fear not, child. My devourer comes. Together we will feast on you and that bitch. The hour is here. She will arrive before dawn."

The ground trembled beneath his feet as he marched in the direction of Nia. Each footprint hissed, steam rising from the scorched earth. The cemetery recoiled, the grass wilting, the air thickening with the stench of sulfur.

He sang as he walked, his voice lilting and cruel.

"Here we come, little one... to make you scream. We'll soak your flesh in your own fluids... roast you over and over again... here we come, little one... here we come."

His skin began to split, his smile stretching too wide. Flesh tore, revealing another mouth beneath, with broken teeth glinting in the moonlight.

"To mix your flesh with all the little children we've been saving for you," he crooned. "Here we come, little Nia. Here we come."

He reached the road and scanned the horizon, locking onto the distant glow of Nia's home. His grin widened, with his lips cracking and bleeding. He sniffed the air like a hound.

"Come to me, my sinners," he whispered. "Come to me." His feet carried him along the road as if he were in no hurry.

The watcher moved ahead of the demon he followed and changed himself into a massive white snowy owl. He had still been given no instructions, and so his duty to watch Eya remained. For the first time in many millennia, he had been allowed to do something on his own, and he would not squander the opportunity. His wings lifted him into the air, and off he flew to leave the demons to their journey.

The humid air clung to Nia's skin. The moon hung low, its pale light fractured by the skeletal branches outside the window. Shadows stretched long across the floor of her living room, twitching as if alive.

Eya's deep voice cut through the silence. "Be prepared. The demon is almost here."

Nia looked up, her breath visible in the sudden chill. "I've prayed for my parents' safety. I know you had something to do with them leaving for that work function. Thank you. Now all that's left is to face this thing... and protect the souls it wants to devour."

Eya nodded, her eyes glowing. "You've been chosen for a divine task, not to prove your strength, but to reveal the truth. Those who stand against you tonight stand against Father, and they will be judged."

She gestured to the staff. "This is not a weapon. It is a mirror. It focuses your faith and reflects it on those who fear it. Like Moses's staff, it was never the power, only the symbol. The children needed something to see, but you... You must believe. You focus on your faith and let the demon be distracted by the staff. Do you understand?"

Nia's fingers tightened around the haft. "So, my training is to watch for the eyes of evil, but true faith... they'll never understand it."

Eya stood, her smile was warm. "Amen."

The girl tapped the smooth end twice against the floor, and with each strike, a drumbeat resonated in the stillness.

"Let's continue."

She knelt again, laying the staff beside her, and bowed her head in prayer. Eya's expression softened.

A gentle rapping began at the window.

Eya moved to the curtains, parting them with care. She did not hesitate to unlock the window and raise it. A rush of cool air swept in.

The hummingbird darted in first. The bees came

buzzing in tight spirals, butterflies and moths fluttered close behind. Crawling creatures followed: caterpillars, spiders, mice, their tiny feet whispering across the floorboards.

They gathered around Nia, forming a living circle. They did not move or make a sound, but they watched. They seemed to understand she was praying.

With a rush of wind and a whisper of feathers, a great snowy owl glided in and landed on the couch. Its wings stretched again almost the length of the furniture before tucking onto its back. It hooted and hissed, its beak snapping in a specific pattern: once, twice, then rapidly, its guttural cries sounding urgent.

Eya approached the owl, her brow furrowed in concern. The archangel listened to the large bird's hisses and hoots. She glanced at the clock.

"Almost 3 a.m. The darkness is near. Be ready, Nia. Let faith be your shield. Let Father be your sword."

Nia rose, her heart steady. "I'm ready, but all of you, go. Find safety."

The girl gripped the staff and stepped outside, and into the street, her bare feet brushing against the cool pavement. She scanned the road, but there was no movement, no sound.

With her eyes closed, she said quietly. "Jesus... help me."

From nowhere and everywhere, a whisper curled around her ear.

"Father said humans have dominion over all things on Earth. All it must do... is be named."

Her eyes snapped open, and she tapped the staff five times, each strike louder than the last. The thundering sound echoed through the neighborhood, vibrating the windows and stirring the leaves.

The world responded. Grass straightened. Flowers

bloomed. Trees rustled with unseen wind. Animals emerged. Foxes, raccoons, and birds watched from a respectable distance.

There was a pinch on her toes. Kana and Nox had latched onto her feet, their claws clamped tight, their tails raised.

"I couldn't ask for better friends," she whispered. "I hope you're ready."

They swung their tails and released their claws and spread their tiny legs to grip her.

Nia said, "I guess we are in this together."

A cold blew past her, but it was not wind. It was as if warmth were absent. A frozen void that swept across the street.

A melodic and beautiful voice sang.

"Hello, little children… I've come to take you away… come little children… to taste your flesh for a thousand years… and then I will do it again… hello, little children… your suffering is my pleasure… and we'll do it again for a thousand years…"

From the shadows, a figure emerged from under a tree. A grotesque naked woman with her smile splitting her face in half. The monstrous woman's teeth were jagged and oversized. Her body was massive, towering over Nia, her skin slick and pale, her limbs too long, too thick.

The demon stopped at the edge of the moonlight, her face cloaked in shadow, save for the mouth. Her voice boomed, feminine and monstrous at the same time.

"Hello, little Nia. I've come a long way to claim you. Do you like what you see? Because I like what I see… my sustenance… my pleasure… I will devour you over and over again for my painful pleasures."

Nia did not flinch. "I guess you're here to be destroyed."

From the porch, Eya leapt, her body a blur of light and fury. The archangel landed beside Nia, her breath calm, her eyes burning with emotion.

Her face had changed. It was no longer serene, but wrathful. A storm rolled in her eyes, and Nia knew that hell was nothing compared to Heaven's wrath. Nothing could survive her fury.

Eya's voice was clear and firm. "We are ready," she said. "Are you?"

The demon laughed. "Ready? I've been ready for centuries. I'll eat your flesh, rip your bowels out, and wear them as a cloak."

She raised her arms and screamed. "I am your fate! Your end! The beginning of your suffering!"

From her chest, steaming black sludge erupted. It was thick and filled with bone fragments and shredded flesh. The ooze pooled and bubbled around her feet. From it, two deformed and serpentine creatures slithered forth, the size of New York City rats. Their mouths were lined with rows of needle-like teeth.

They crawled toward Nia, their eyes glowing and hypnotic. They were made of sludge and bones, fit together oddly, and resembled snakes.

The demon savored the moment. A smile crept up her cheeks as she waited to see the fear in the little girl.

Nia smiled a crooked, knowing smile as if she understood a joke that nobody else had understood.

"I see you brought help. So did I."

The evil creature sneered. "Your pet Angel? She's no threat. I'll take her power after I take your life."

The monsters paused, ready to strike. Kana and Nox leapt on the serpents' heads, their stingers flashing with constant strikes in seconds. The creatures twisted and shrieked, but they were flesh now. Subject to Earth's laws.

They could not escape. The demon stared, her grin faltering. The snake-like creatures fell still as the venom spread through their misshapen heads.

Two insignificant scorpions had undone her beasts.

The monster took a step forward, the ground beneath its feet sizzling with each contact, leaving behind scorched craters that hissed with rising steam. Its voice slithered through the air.

"How dare your vermin attack my pets?"

Its eyes, once hidden behind a mask of human beauty, now glowed with a sickly amber light. The flesh around its mouth twitched, blistering with rage. The demon did not appear angry, but instead seemed shocked that its creations, born of bile and bone, could be undone by such insignificant creatures.

Eya knelt, her robes brushing the dew-slick grass, and scooped up Kana and Nox. Their armored bodies shimmered in the moonlight.

"Fool," she said, her voice calm but edged with steel. "Don't concern yourself with my friends. Worry about yourself."

She pressed her lips to their carapaces, and they responded with a soft scrape of claws against her cheek. She walked to the side of the yard and placed them in the grass.

"Thank you both for your courage," she whispered. "Carry the knowledge that Nia will be your friend forever. Until we meet again."

The demon's body trembled, its tall and heavy form rippling with fury. The air around it grew heavier, the essence of sulfur and rotting meat growing stronger. It stared after the archangel, growling at her back.

The creature stopped approaching. "What?" it hissed. "Did you think they were my only pets?"

It raised a clawed finger, jagged and blackened, and

pointed at Nia. With a sickening squelch, it dragged the claw down its own abdomen, slicing open its stomach with a wet, tearing sound. The wound gaped, revealing glistening coils of serpentine intestines that slithered out.

The moment they hit the ground, a low buzzing began. It was soft at first, as if it were the distant hum of bees. The sound grew until it was deafening.

The intestines bloated, before bursting in a spray of black ichor. From within, a swarm erupted thousands of grotesque flies, each the size of a thumb, their wings serrated, their mouths lined with jagged teeth. They circled the demon, and the air was vibrating with a choir of hunger.

"Devour them all!" she roared.

Before the swarm could descend, the sound of rhythmic flapping wings rose over the buzzing. Nia and Eya did not flinch. Their smiles were quiet, knowing.

A sharp clicking filled the air. The hummingbird shot past Nia's face, its wings brushing her cheek with a whisper of wind. A second later, a torrent, sparrows, crows, and hawks burst forth from the trees and dark skies, followed by a cloud of bats, their leathery forms slicing through the night.

The swarm of flies scattered, shrieking in high-pitched clicks, but the bats were faster. They tore through the flies, devouring them midair. Feathers and wings collided in a frenzy of motion and sound.

The demon screamed a guttural, bone-rattling roar that echoed across the neighborhood. Windows cracked. Dogs howled. The last of the minions were consumed or scattered in a matter of seconds.

Nia raised her hand, and her flying allies swooped close, brushing her fingertips with feathers and wings like a high-five gesture of unity.

The demon's face twisted, the human mask blistering,

peeling in patches. Its eyes widened with a feeling it must not have felt in centuries: fear.

"No!" it shrieked. "I cannot be denied! In Hell, I am feared! I am hated! My playthings worship me with their hate!"

Eya stood still, her arms folded, her expression serene.

The demon's fury boiled over at the sight of the archangel, seemingly uninterested in the events before her.

"I will feast upon you before the sun crests the mountains!" it bellowed.

Its smile tore wider, splitting its face nearly in two. The demon charged at them, its body a blur, its feet barely touching the ground.

Nia raised the staff and slammed it into the pavement.

A resounding boom rippled outward. The air trembled. The evil being paused mid-stride, its body shuddering. No leaves stirred. No echoes rang.

The demon snarled. "Did you think a splinter could summon the power to destroy me? I am the tormentor of tormentors! I am your eternity!"

It lunged again.

Eya stepped forward; her voice was thunder.

"You are nothing compared to Nia, and you are nothing compared to me. I am Eya. You are an insignificant speck of useless ash. I've heard your boasts before from Zar. Adam Monroe destroyed her. Ever heard of him?"

The demon's voice dropped to a growl as it froze again. "Yes. She was my daughter. I fed her her first flesh. I raised her. I am her creator. I am Xaxan, master of Hell!"

Eya stepped back, her eyes meeting Nia's. She winked.

Nia smiled, raised the staff again, and hurled it with all her strength. It sliced the air, aimed straight for Xaxan's eye.

The demon caught it mid-flight, gripping it with ease. Deliberately, it lowered the shaft of wood with a sneer.

"Did you think this could stop me? Hurt me? Kill me? You're pathetic, you piece of shit."

Nia's voice was calm. "It's not meant to hurt you. It's meant to hold you."

Xaxan's face twisted in confusion. "What are you talking…"

Vines erupted from the staff, wrapping around Xaxan's arm, its torso, and its legs in a flash. The monster screamed, thrashing, but the vines grew thicker, stronger, binding it with chains forged from the earth itself.

"No! No! I am the most powerful demon in Hell! I've devoured flesh, bones, souls! How is this splinter binding me? How does it hold me back from my meal?"

Nia stepped forward. "You are powerful in Hell, but you're not in Hell. You're on Earth. In human form, and here, you are subject to Father's laws for all humankind, even the ones like you." She raised her voice. "Father said that to defeat evil, you must call it by name. Hello, Xaxan."

The demon's eyes widened, its mouth slack. It had given up its name. It had sealed its fate.

It shrieked, "Come to me, lover! Your master calls! Free me from this toothpick! I will kill the Angel! I will kill the meat flesh!"

The black sludge around it bubbled and boiled, forming a cloud of steam that hovered and pulsed.

BOOM!

The cloud exploded, spewing gore across the yard.

From the center of the blast, another figure emerged.

It was a naked middle-aged man, but Nia knew he was no man under the flesh. The skin sloughed off the demon in thick, melted plops.

The demon stood five feet tall, but its presence was suffocating. Its body was a grotesque lattice of exposed black bone and dripping meat, each sinew glistening with thick, red globs that hissed as they hit the ground. The air around it reeked of rot and iron, like a butcher's floor left to fester.

Its smile stretched wide, teeth gleaming. "Hello, Nia," it rasped, voice wet and gurgling. "I see you've met my father. Let him go… or never mind. I'll do it myself. Then we'll both lick the blood off your bones after we devour your delicious flesh."

Nia and Eya stood motionless, watching as the creature turned. Its fingers elongated into thin, bony blades that blazed with a sickly sheen. With a single swipe, it sliced through the vines of the staff that bound Xaxan. It sliced repeatedly, cutting more vines each time.

The staff groaned, trying to hold, but the damage was done. Xaxan pulled free, his feminine body rippling with dark energy. The two demons laughed in unison, their deep, guttural sound vibrating the bones of the earth.

"We're going to enjoy your flesh," they hissed, "sooooually and deliciously… over and over again. Through centuries. Through never-ending screams."

Nia's eyes narrowed. "Impossible. You're an unworthy minion, and I'll kill Xaxan after I destroy you."

The smaller demon snarled. "I am not a minion! I am RRuraZ, master of Hell! I am thy death! That is my name, remember it well!"

Xaxan glared at the smaller demon. "Idiot!"

Nia's lips curled into a sly smile. "Gotcha. RRuraZ, you and your master are as dumb as you are ugly. Now I know both your names."

She plucked a strand of Eya's hair. It was silver, radiant, and humming with divine energy. With a whip of her arm, she lashed it forward. The strand shot out, wrapping around RRuraZ, binding him in a tense cocoon of light.

RRuraZ shrieked, its voice cracking. "What is happening?! Eya, your God,... your angels... aren't allowed to interfere!"

Nia's voice was steel. "Eya didn't interfere. I did. I took her hair. Nothing was given. So shut up and be destroyed."

She sprinted forward, her feet pounding the earth as Xaxan gripped the threads binding the smaller demon and reached for Nia with another massive, clawed hand. Nia twisted around the hand and grabbed a shard of her staff, its surface warm to the touch. She closed her eyes. A tear slipped from her left eye, landing on the shard.

It glowed with a soft blue light, radiating from it. The girl plunged it into RRuraZ's skull and spun to drive it into Xaxan's face.

Both demons froze in place, no longer crying or making any more obscene threats.

Their bodies collapsed and melted into themselves, dripping onto the road in puddles of black ichor. The staff clattered to the ground.

A black flame erupted from the remains, roaring skyward. It burned with no heat and no smoke. The smell of rain was in the breeze. Thunder rolled across the hills. A flash of lightning split the sky. The rain came softly at first, then grew steadily heavier. It felt like a blessing, washing away the filth and extinguishing the unholy fire. Nia turned to Eya.

Eya stood with her arms raised, her silhouette framed by the storm light.

"Miracles," she said, "are given by Father when asked. He always answers. Sometimes he says no. This time... He said yes."

Nia smiled, her shoulders sagging with relief. She

walked to the staff, lifted it, and turned to leave.

A shadow rose behind her, growing seven feet tall, stretching across the pavement. It reformed into the woman-shaped horror. The demon's flesh was barely stitched together by rage and defiance.

She laughed. "Did you think I'd be destroyed that easily? I am a knight of the highest demons in Hell!"

Nia stopped. Eya's eyes locked onto hers. "I had hoped," The girl said. "But don't worry. I'll finish it now."

Eya's voice was ice. "Fool. You should've returned to the pit. Here, you are weak, and now, it's too late."

Nia spun, slashing with the sharpened staff. Xaxan blocked. She struck again and again, each blow ringing with fury. The demon countered, but Nia was faster. The shaft parried the claw and slapped against her neck. She followed with a kick to the knee.

When the demon staggered, she drove the staff upward, piercing its abdomen. Nia pushed, gritting her teeth, until the end burst through the top of its skull.

Xaxan's scream was a guttural, choking noise.

It slumped, but the staff held firm, driving deeper. Ichor sprayed into the wind and evaporated.

The body dissolved, and the earth opened, swallowing the remains and the staff. Within a few seconds, grass grew and flowers bloomed in its place.

Nia dropped to her knees, gasping for breath. Her body trembled, her soul stretched thin.

Eya had witnessed the battle to see how the young girl carried herself. To see if she was ready. She raised her hands to Heaven and leapt ten feet into the air, landing where Xaxan had died. A boom echoed, shaking the neighborhood.

The sun broke the horizon. Golden light bathed their faces.

Nia looked at Eya. "I guess this is goodbye?"

Eya smiled. "You have a choice to make. Choose wisely. From me and all your new friends, choose what is best for you."

The archangel shimmered, turning to silver dust. The sunlight caught it, scattering glitter across the yard.

Nia's tears fell, but her smile remained. Eya had been forgiven. She had returned to Heaven.

She closed her eyes and turned her head to the sky. The sun warmed her face.

A flutter brushed her ear. Nia did not need to look, as she raised her hands and cupped them. The hummingbird landed in her palms, cocking its head.

"What's your name?"

She stared at the small bird as if she were listening to some unheard voice.

"Oh, really? Fig? I never would've guessed. You have a wonderful name. You can be my helper."

Fig flew to her shoulder as Nia turned toward home.

Eya's voice echoed, fading. "Well, Nia… you will fare well. Father is with you."

I want to thank all those who have enjoyed my writing of My Imagination. You have seen a drop of what my mind is capable of creating when I am not trying. So please tell yourself that this is not real. Tell yourself over and over again that it is all imaginary. Again, thank you for joining me, and see you in the darkness of my mind. I, J.P. ALBA, thank you.

Discover More Stories from Shield Blade Publishing

From TL Jeffcoat
Flames of the Devil Dog

Colonel Enzo Montanue, once the crown's deadliest weapon, led his Devil Dogs through rebellions, monsters, and rogue mages. But when betrayal shatters his loyalty and endangers his family, he's thrust into a shadow war of vengeance and secrets. As the kingdom rots from within, Enzo must choose—save what remains or let the Devil Dogs' legacy burn.

Available now on Amazon Kindle, Hardcover, & Paperback.

Stay Connected
Explore more titles at
- **https://sbpub.great-site.net/**

Follow us on Facebook:
- **https://www.facebook.com/ShieldBladePublishing**